TALES OF
a heaux

NATISHA RAYNOR

Natisha Raynor

© 2021

All rights reserved. No part of this book may be reproduced or transmitted in any form or by any means, electric or mechanical, including photocopying, recording, or by any information storage and retrieval system without the written permission from the publisher or author, except for the inclusion of brief quotations in a review.

This is a work of fiction. It is not meant to depict, portray or represent any particular real persons. All the characters, incidents and dialogues are the product of the author's imagination and are not to be constructed as real. Any resemblance to actual events or person living or dead is purely coincidental.

Suzon ♥

    The ridiculously thick bottle girl came back over to my section with two bottles of 1942 in her hands. The expensive tequila that was dressed up in the pretty bottle was a very hot commodity in the club. Our server's body, the bottles with lit sparklers in them, and all of the bad bitches and rich niggas in my section had the attention of everyone in the club. People were out in abundance partying in memory of my ex-boyfriend, Big Draco. It had been one year since some pussies had murdered him and left thousands of people to mourn him. Big Draco had hoes for sure. I mean, he was a twenty-four year old successful rapper, but I was the one that got posted on his social media. I was the one that got taken on the road with him, and I met his family. I was his chick. His main. The other broads were just something for him to do on the side. The women he ran to in order to make himself feel like that nigga.

    I fucked with Big Draco for a little over a year, but he didn't start posting me until two months before his death. Had he not started doing that, I would be just another groupie claiming to have been stroked by Big Draco's eight inch dick. He was the one that put me out there, and that shit changed my life. Big Draco introduced me to a whole new world. One that I refused to leave, but I had to move strategically. Please understand when I say I miss the fuck out of him. But life has to go on and me playing the role of the grieving girlfriend is working in my favor. Take for instance, this celebration. I was invited by one of Big Draco's labelmates. I got in for free of course, and I was partying with some of the hottest rappers in the industry all in the name of Big Draco.

    The first time Big Draco posted me it made it to the Shaderoom. One of the most popular gossip blogs on IG. With more than a million followers, that blog can make your ass or break you. From there, I got more than ten thousand followers, and I started capitalizing off that shit right away. People started sending me free products to promote and not only do I promote them, but I charge crazy prices to do so. To post a product on my page for twenty-four hours, I charge $700. For forty-eight hours, I charge $1,200. On a good week, I can earn around $4,500 just from that. I've also been asked to do a few club hostings, and I get paid from when I go live on IG because so many people join the live. My most popular live had around 27,000 views. I gained that much popularity from being the girlfriend of a rapper. It was insane! I've also gotten checks from Tik Tok because a lot of my videos I made with Big Draco before he died go viral. I know my lil' fifteen minutes of fame can be over real damn fast, so I'm trying my best to use it to my advantage for as long as I can.

    One of his songs came on, and I immediately turned up for the crowd. I really did miss him, but Big Draco wasn't coming back. I couldn't grieve myself back to the slums. I had to make something shake, and the money that I was getting off of his popularity was the fastest way for me to get money besides becoming a scammer, a drug dealer, a stripper, or an escort.

"One time for the homie Big Draco! Rest in heaven my G!" The DJ shouted into the mic as I poured a shot of liquor.

I'm not all that familiar with heaven but if there is one, I doubt Big Draco's ass is there. He rapped about bodies and the people that knew him for real, knew it wasn't cap. Big Draco had raised a lot of hell in his time on Earth. If he fucked with you, then you were always good but if he was your enemy, you'd better watch over your shoulder at all times. He was one of a kind. He wasn't the tallest in fact, he was the shortest man that I ever dated, but I loved all 5 feet 9 inches of him. I loved his cocoa colored skin and his stark white teeth. One of the very few rappers in the game without veneers that had an award winning smile. He told me his mom worked three jobs for six months straight to be able to afford braces for him when he was twelve. He didn't want to wear them, but he beat any nigga's ass that tried to clown him. Seeing how hard his mother worked for those braces made him learn to appreciate them.

Big Draco's homie, Papi passed me a blunt, and I hit it a few times. When Big Draco first passed, I had to be high all the time in order not to be hysterical. The life that I live doesn't exactly call for sobriety. Getting paid to party, traveling, doing photo shoots, I can be high as a kite and still do what I needed to do. Even though, I still had tried to cut back just a bit. I for damn sure didn't spend too much of my money on the shit, but if it was being given to me then cool.

By the time the club closed, I was lit but thankfully, my hotel room wasn't far away. I'm from Charlotte, North Carolina, and Big Draco was from Memphis, Tennessee. This particular party was in New

York however, so I came down for the weekend.

"I think this is my Uber," I said to my friend Mona. Mona was a God send for me. I met her through Big Draco. She was fucking with his man, and Mona is a hoe, but she's plugged in. Being cool with her puts me in some dope ass positions.

"Okay babe. Text me when you get to the room. I love you," she had a lazy grin on her face, and I knew it was from all of the coke and liquor that she had consumed. Mona was a party girl for sure, and she was with whatever.

"I love you too boo." My grin was probably just as lazy as hers, but I felt lovely as hell. All the free liquor and weed had me on cloud nine. I always chose not to indulge in any other kind of drugs.

I got inside the Uber, said my hellos, and hoped that the driver wouldn't be in a talking mood. Luckily for me she wasn't, and I just scrolled through my phone while I rode to my destination. At the hotel, I got on the elevator and pressed the button with the number 7 on it. I peered at my long, white, coffin shaped nail and made a mental note to get a fill-in as soon as I touched back down in Charlotte. Inside the hotel room, I kicked my shoes off instantly and headed in the bathroom. I grabbed a make-up wipe and cleaned the make-up from my honey colored skin. I then pulled my long weave up into a messy bun and peeled my skintight white dress from my thick frame.

After a quick shower, I was in the middle of putting lotion on when there was a knock on the door. I already knew who it was and what they wanted, so I didn't even cover up. I'm only 5'4, so I had to stand on my tip toes to see out of the peephole. I pulled the door open, and Papi strolled inside of the room while his eyes slid up and down my body. He kept his eyes trained on me as he kicked his designer sneakers off then pulled his shirt over his head.

"Put that ass in the air," he demanded in a low voice as he unbuckled his belt ready to get straight to business.

I was drunk, high, and horny, so I didn't hesitate to do what he asked, but if I thought about it too hard, I would feel bad. If people could turn over in their graves for real, I knew that Big Draco for sure would be. Him and Papi had been tight for years. They were mad close, and nine months after Big Draco's death, me and Papi started fucking. I didn't plan on it. He used to just keep in touch and check on me at first. Then, he invited me to one of his shows my birthday weekend, and he gave me $5,000. I got super fucked up, and when he made a move on me, I didn't object. The sex turned out to be great, and we'd been rocking ever since.

I let out a soft moan when I felt Papi's mouth on my mound. The arch in my back deepened, and I slowly twerked my ass on his face as he sucked and slurped on my pussy from behind. "Papiiiii," his name escaped my throat in a soft whisper as I cupped my left breast in my hand and enjoyed the way he was devouring me.

He loved when I moaned his name. That shit made him go harder with the licking and sucking and when he stuck a finger gently inside my ass, the dam broke. I grabbed a fistful of sheets as I moaned loud as hell. My body jerked against his face, and he still didn't take his lips off me. "Got damn Papi, fuck!" I cried out as he probed his tongue deeper into my pussy.

I was breathing hard as hell, and I even pounded my fist on the bed, but he didn't let up. I was making all kinds of weird noises and whimpering softly as he explored my sensitive clit with his tongue. By the time he removed his mouth, all I could do was collapse on the bed, and that made him snicker.

"Turn that ass over," he gently demanded as he got undressed.

It took every ounce of energy that I had, but I did it. Once I was flat on my back and staring up into his handsome face, I took in the smirk that he wore. Papi was light-skinned with green eyes and long hair that he had managed to loc up despite how soft and fine it was. I'm not sure what he's mixed with, but I've seen pictures of his mother, and she's a gorgeous dark-skinned woman. Not sure if his father is just light-skin or of another race. It really doesn't even matter. This shit with Papi was never supposed to go as far as it did, but it was too late to turn back.

After the condom was secured on his dick, he slid into me forcefully before covering my lips with his. He snaked his tongue into my mouth, and we shared a sloppy tongue kiss that allowed the sweet taste of my own juices to find its' way into my mouth. I moaned into his mouth as we kissed, and he savagely stroked my walls.

"Papi," I moaned his stage name for the third time while I threw my head back, locked my legs around his waist, and grabbed his locs. His dick wasn't all that big, but he always made me cum, and I've had some guys with big dicks that didn't even make me cum.

"Yeah, say that shit." Me calling his name always stroked his ego.

"You feel so good, Papi," I stared into his eyes before kissing him.

Papi sucked on my neck, my nipple, then my bottom lip as he stroked me. It didn't take too long before he was letting out a loud deep moan and shooting his load into the condom that he wore. Papi rolled off me and headed into the bathroom to clean off. When he was done, he placed money on the dresser like he always did, kissed me on the lips, and left. I glanced over at the money while exhaling deeply. Money was always the motive, but I couldn't help but feel like I was moving foul as fuck. I mean, I was. Papi was Big Draco's right hand man. I knew he was cheating on me and me moving on wouldn't be the worst thing in the world, *but* I had moved on with his friend. His best friend.

On top of that, Papi is married. So, there are plenty of reasons why no one can ever find out about us. I grabbed the money and counted it. Papi had not only paid for my hotel room and my flight, but he had also just blessed me with $4,000. It was about to be May 1st, and as soon as I got back to North Carolina, I was using some of that to pay my rent. Since I'm so well known for being with Big Draco, I have to stay in a secure location, and my high rise condo isn't cheap. Every month that I'm able to pay my rent is a blessing, and I have to thank God for it. I can't let my popularity from being with Big Draco go to waste. As soon as it's safe for me to move on, meaning I won't be judged by the public, I have to find a nigga that's on the same level or even larger than Big Draco was. My main mission was to secure that muhfuckin' bag.

ESAI 🏀

"Nigga, we really 5-0 out this muhfucka. It's about to be a lovely season!" My teammate Bakari was hype as hell. We had won our fifth game of the season against the New York Knicks, and we were happy as hell.

We were having a little celebration at a club out in New York, but I knew I couldn't party too hard. I had a 6 am flight and in two days, we had a home game against the Detroit Pistons. It wasn't the time to slack off, and I had to make sure to be on my A game, and that meant not drinking too much and staying away from weed or any other drugs. I was in my prime. Three years in the NBA, and I'm worth a cool $12,000,000.

"Facts!" I gave him dap and took the shot he extended towards me.

I threw it back and observed my surroundings. Right beside us, there was a group of rappers and industry cats partying in celebration of one of my favorite rappers, Big Draco. A few of them had come over and shown me and my teammates love, and that's an indescribable feeling. I've loved basketball since before I could talk good. It was really my life, and it felt good to be recognized for doing something that I love. I bobbed my head to the music and watched as the few females in the section with the rappers twerked and turned up. Bakari followed my gaze.

"Big Draco's girl is fine as hell, and I think her body real 'cus them thighs match like a muhfucka. She built like a got damn stallion."

"That she is," I appreciated the beautiful woman.

I didn't know her or much about her except from what I saw and heard, but I knew the females she was with were straight up sack chasers. Since being a pro athlete, I've been astounded at some of the things that women will actually do not even just for money but to be with an athlete period. Every time I think I've seen it all, some more shit comes out that I'm shocked by. One of my teammates just got put on blast by a groupie that said he paid her $1,500 to shit on him. Yeah, you heard that right. She said he asked her to defecate on him. Of course, he said it's not true, but some people do have weird sick ass fetishes. I don't know which one of them is the most disgusting. The woman that did the shit or the man that wanted it done.

Me and my girl, Afrika have been together for the past nine years. We started dating our junior year in high school. I'll never front like I've been faithful to her the entire time we've been together, but my cheating doesn't so much come from me being famous. It comes from us having been together for so long, and me just wanting to feel some new pussy. It's wrong, but I'm being honest. I've cheated on her with about thirteen different women, but in nine years, I don't see that as terrible. A few of them were in my college days, but I love Afrika, and it's been almost a year since I cheated. I don't want to be that guy that shits on the girl that was down for him when he was broke to be with a groupie or someone that has been passed around.

My phone vibrated in my hand, and I looked

down to see a notification from the security app I have installed on my phone. Afrika and I aren't married, but she of course lives in my million dollar house with me. I'm not ready for kids just yet. We're still in the traveling, having spontaneous sex, and enjoying being rich phase. We might start talking about it in another year, but whenever we do have kids, we'll be more than prepared. My house has eight bedrooms, five bathrooms, a movie room, a gym, and an indoor basketball court. When I'm home, I spend majority of my time in the gym, basketball court, or the movie room. Afrika was a little scared to stay home alone when we first moved in, but I have top of the line security equipment plus a huge ass gate that seals my crib off from outsiders. My first year in the league, she traveled with me often but now, not so much. She makes sure to attend every home game though.

 With furrowed brows, I tapped the icon to see what was going on. It was after midnight, so I doubted Afrika was leaving the house. I narrowed my eyes as I zeroed in on the footage from my living room and saw someone walking through the front door. Afrika was dressed in a black lace teddy, and the nigga that entered the crib, wasted no time kissing and rubbing on her. It felt as if I'd been punched in the gut, and my mind started to reel. I had to be seeing shit. I had to be. Not only was another man in my house kissing on my bitch, but I knew the nigga. It was my best friend, Tyrese.

 All I could do was stare at my phone screen, and the more I watched, the angrier I became. My girlfriend and my homie were making out like long lost lovers that had just been reunited. This couldn't be happening. It was bad enough that Afrika was cheating, but it couldn't be with my friend. It couldn't be. It had to be someone that looked just like him. My blood felt as if it was literally boiling. My body temperature even rose, and that's not a good feeling to have when you're in a packed ass nightclub. I had to go outside and get some air. I felt like I was going to throw up the few shots that I had consumed. I know I've cheated on Afrika before. Plenty of times, but this shit was out of pocket. In my house? With my best friend? She had lost her muhfuckin' mind. I had never put my hands on a woman before, but all I could see were visions of me choking the shit out of her.

  The fact that I was all the way in New York was literally saving her life. I guess it's true what they say. Men can dish that shit out, but we can't take it. I was gripping my phone so tight in my hand that my fingers were starting to hurt. I punched in the code to unlock my phone, and I called the one person that I knew could make this shit right until I could get home.

  "Hello?" my younger sister, Veronica answered the phone in a lazy voice.

  "You sleep?" I asked with my adrenaline pumping.

  "Nah, sitting here scrolling through Tik Tok. What's up?"

  "I just saw on my security footage that Tyrese is at my crib. Afrika is cheating on me with that nigga, and I want you to go beat her ass and drag her out my shit."

  "Say less."

  One thing I love about my sister is that she has my back with no questions asked. I knew that she would go and do exactly what I had just told her to do.

  I didn't even sleep. I left the club, headed straight back to my hotel room and grabbed my shit. I caught an Uber to the airport and did everything in my power to get an earlier flight. The only flight I could catch left out a four, so I stayed at the airport for two hours before I boarded the plane. Four hours and an Uber ride later, I was pulling up at my house, and I saw Veronica's Benz and Afrika's Audi R8. I really hoped that Veronica had done what I asked because if Afrika was still there, I couldn't be in control of what I might do. When I entered the house, Veronica was stretched out on my couch asleep. The long strands of weave scattered on the floor, told me that there had been a fight.

"Yo," I called out with my nostrils flaring. I was suddenly angry all over again.

Veronica opened her eyes and stretched. I had given her a spare key to my house when I first moved in and thank God I had. She'd never used it, but it came in handy on this night. Veronica sat up and shook her head. "I caught them. In your bed. That bitch really tried it. I dragged her off his ass, but I couldn't even beat her like I wanted to because hoe ass Tyrese broke it up. While he was getting dressed, I ran down here and got my keys. I pepper sprayed the fuck out his ass and while he couldn't see, I beat her ass all over this living room. By the time I was done, one of her eyes was swollen shut. I dragged her ass out on the porch and left her there. I thought she might call the police, but she hasn't so far. All of her shit is still here. Even her phone. I put her out in nothing but her robe."

For as hurt and mad as I was, her story brought me a small sense of joy. I knew she would come through for me. We were raised in the suburbs, but Veronica played no games. Sometimes, I get the feeling that she enjoys having to whoop a bitch. Once I started making real money, I was determined to be smart with it, and I opened a commercial cleaning company. The monthly profit I make from that goes straight to my retirement fund. I let Veronica run it, and she's very professional when she needs to be. Shit, I pay her $150,000 a year to run the shit, so she better be professional. However, she will still check a muhfucka when needed. She's gonna ride for me regardless, but the fact that she used to fuck with Tyrese probably had her going extra hard on Afrika.

I sat down on the couch. The entire moment felt surreal. Nine years gone down the drain. How long had she been cheating on me? She has a degree in Medical Billing and Coding. For the past few months, Afrika had been in the process of starting her own company, but it wasn't up and running. Ever since she graduated from college, I've been taking care of her. I give her an allowance of $3,500 a month, plus I pay all the bills, and she has access to my credit and bank cards. Just the month before, I bought that hoe a $17,000 Birkin bag. Just thinking about the shit had me clenching my teeth and breathing like a damn bull. And Tyrese? That had been my nigga since middle school. I gave that bitch ass nigga $5,000 for his birthday. I was ready to murder something. I stood up.

"Tyrese 'bout to see me."

Veronica jumped up. "Esai, no. Trust me, he deserves an ass whooping, and he knows it. But if you pull up to his house, that man is not going to open the door. He might even call the police, and you don't need to risk getting into trouble for him. You have that meeting with Nike coming up for a $1,000,000 endorsement. I know it sounds easy for me to say but *fuck that nigga*. Let them two scandalous muhfuckas have each other. He for damn sure can't take care of her the way you did. That nigga puts medication in boxes." Veronica frowned up her face like she had tasted something funny.

Tyrese worked at a pharmaceutical plant, and he makes like $23 an hour. A lot of people would kill for that kind of pay but compared to me, he for damn sure couldn't take care of Afrika the way I did. I never tried to stunt on Tyrese or make him feel bad, and I've bought that nigga countless pairs of designer shoes, clothes, I even copped him a Rolex one year for Christmas, took him on numerous vacations with me, and this is how he did me? I was tempted to ignore Veronica's words of caution, but I listened. Instead of leaving to go fuck Tyrese up, I took the stairs two at a time. I wasn't worried about practice or my upcoming game. I spent hours going through Veronica's things. I could have been a cruddy nigga and not let her take anything, but I wasn't even gon' do all that. One thing about Afrika, she didn't just wear designer. So, all her basic shit, I packed up for her.

The designer shit though, the bags and the shoes, the jewelry and the expensive clothes, they were staying at my crib. She wasn't taking any of that with her and whatever she had in the bank, I hoped it was enough to last. While I was at the airport waiting on my flight, I locked my accounts, so she couldn't get any money off my cards or from the ATM. The things I was letting her keep, I put them out on the porch, then I called a locksmith to have my locks changed. Fuck Afrika's hoe ass.

Suzon ♥

"Damn Sue. You be acting like you don't fuck with the hood no more," my mother's neighbor Po Boy said as I headed up the sidewalk to her door.

"I just be busy. How you doing though?" I really didn't give a fuck, but folks love to holla that a person is stuck up. I wouldn't say I'm stuck up. More like smart. My mom lives in the trenches. Picture me hanging out there and "fucking with the hood" for them same niggas to try and rob me or some shit. I don't even wear my jewelry when I visit my mom.

And I rarely stay more than twenty minutes at a time. Me and my mom have never been close, and we never will be. What she calls giving tough love and keeping it real, I call toxic and abusive. My mother loves pointing out my imperfections. Whether she's telling me to stop drinking sodas 'cus it's fucking up my skin, or calling my nose big, even saying I dress like a hoe. She'd rather eat shit than give me a compliment and because of it, my self-esteem is low as fuck. Strangers can tell me I'm pretty all day, and I won't believe that shit. I've even had family members tell me that my mother is jealous of me. How in the hell are you jealous of your own child? That shit is beyond me.

The only time she's halfway nice to me is when she needs something. My mom is a waitress, and she makes just enough to cover her $100 rent and her other little bills. Her car is a lemon, and she's always hollering broke. Even though I don't fuck with her like that, I help her out some just because I'm in the position to do so, but it's funny to me how the very ones you shit on might be the ones you need. I looked around at the trash on the ground and the kids running around playing. The hood wasn't all bad, but it was far from good most times, and I never wanted to come back to this shit. People like Po Boy would steal a tooth out your mouth while you were asleep then help you look for the shit. I finesse and get through life the best way I can, but I still don't cross certain lines. I've cracked some credit cards, and I'll sell a lil' pussy to the right person, but I still have more character than a lot of people.

"I've been aight. Waiting on this employment to come through. I'm fucked up right now, but it should be coming any day now."

"Hopefully it will. Let me get in here and holla at my mom." I flashed him a fake smile and got the hell on. I didn't think he'd ask me for money, but you never know. I've had people I haven't seen in years hit me up on social media asking to borrow money. Everybody has a sob story, and I don't have shit for them. Just like before Big Draco came along, nobody had shit for me.

Big Draco bought me a lot of nice shit, and he gave me money, but I wasn't his wife. We didn't live together, and I didn't know the code to his safe. When he died, he had just given me $10,000 the day before, and that was all I had to my name. That and mad designer purses, shoes, clothes, and some jewelry. I didn't want to sell my jewelry, so I had to make those ten stacks last. When that ran out, I cracked a few cards and went up on my promotion prices. If those hosting gigs hadn't come through, I might be assed out by now. Hosting parties at clubs made my following go up even more, and it put extra money in my pocket. In a minute though, nobody will be paying me to come party. They'll be trying to get the newest hottest influencer out there.

When I walked inside my mom's apartment, she was sitting on the couch in her stained Waffle House uniform smoking a cigarette. Her box braids were up in a bun, and she needed to take them out about three weeks ago. Her new growth was something fierce. There was an ever present scowl on her chestnut colored face. My mother could be the poster child for bitter. My father left her when she was five months pregnant and I could be wrong, but I don't think she ever bounced back from that shit. Either that, or something from her past just made her evil as hell. I'm not the only person she was a bitch to and because of that, she never kept a man for long. She had been single for the past ten years or so, and I looked at her as everything I never wanted to be. If she kept her shit up, she was going to die a lonely, mean ass old woman.

She might live in a not so great environment, but her apartment is decorated nice, and she keeps it very clean. When I started dating Big Draco, I knew she probably got her hopes up that I would move her to a house or something, but Big Draco's money wasn't mine. She had never even been to my condo but when I told her the area that I lived in the first thing she did was kiss her teeth then say, *'Tuh. Must be nice.'* For as mean and hateful as she'd always been to me, I'd never feel guilty about not doing more for her. She better be glad I was doing anything.

"Hello," I stated in a dry tone. It's a weird ass feeling to dread even being around your own mother.

Maybeline took a long drag from her cigarette.

Shit, for all I knew, she was pissed that she had to grow up with a name like Maybeline. "I see you're back from New York. You sure be doing a lot of traveling and stuff but every time I say something about moving, you act broke."

This was the shit that got under my skin. "I never said I was broke, but I'm not rich either. I can't be responsible for two rents. My condo costs enough."

"You never even extended the invitation for me to come and stay with you in your little fancy ass condo," she sneered and took another pull from her cigarette. "I guess I'm just supposed to die in the gutter while you out living life."

One thing about it, I don't go out of my way to disrespect my mother, but I'm not a scared little girl anymore. I refused to be afraid to tell her what was on my mind. Still, I kept my voice at a respectful tone. "We've never gotten along. You don't even treat me right, so why would I invite you into my home to disturb my peace?"

My mother's eyes widened, and she jerked her head back. "Ha! Disturb your peace?! Well, excuse the hell out of me. Miss high and mighty. You think you all that, but don't get too cocky. The same way you got all the shit you have now you can lose it all. Don't forget that shit," she smashed her cigarette butt feverishly in the ashtray that sat on her glass coffee table.

I walked over to the same table and placed $300 on it. "There you go and you're welcome." I turned and walked out of the door before she could respond. A simple ass visit always turned into an argument, and I was over the shit. I borderline hated her. The woman that gave me life. If she was going to treat me like shit my entire life, why did she even have me? I guess when my father left her, he left me too, because he didn't have anything to do with me.

    The only people that ever showed me what healthy love looked like were my maternal grandparents. Many times, I asked them if I could live with them, and my mother would always tell me no. I don't even think she really cared for real if I did go live with them, but she just knew it would make me happy. It was as if she wanted me to be angry and miserable right along with her and seeing as how my grandparents were so good to me, I'm baffled at how my mother turned out the way that she did. I got in my red 2018 Lexus and slammed the door. It would be a long ass time before I came back to see her or give her any money. I didn't *have* to help her. At the end of the day, she's a grown ass woman. She could take care of herself and if not, that wasn't my problem. I drove off with a scowl on my face that mirrored the one she always wore. Her toxic ass energy always rubbed off on me. It never failed.

    Minutes later, I had to remind myself to relax the muscles in my face. My phone rang, and I saw that Mona was calling. That lifted my spirits some because she rarely ever called just to bullshit. For small talk, she would comment on one of my IG posts or lives but when she had something worth talking about, she called. Mona has been with about ten different rappers and athletes that I know of. Like me, she gets paid to do hostings and social media promotions. She also has a YouTube channel, and her claim to fame was being in a two-year relationship with an NFL player. When they broke up, she had a slew of clothes, bags, and jewelry. After she moved out of his house, she sold a ring that he bought her and got an apartment and some furniture with the money. By the time the rent was due again, she had moved on to a rapper, and he paid her rent up for six months, took her to Punta Cana, and gifted her with a few bags.

    A lot of people think it's dumb for women that don't have their own money to want pricy bags and shoes, but let me put you up on some free game. Rich niggas will fuck a broke chick, but looking like money attracts money. If a chick is up in the club wearing a $3,000 watch with a $5,000 purse on her shoulder, and she's a bad bitch, other niggas with money will want to fuck with her, and they'll know out the gate she's not gon' fuck for free. And guess what, a lot of niggas with money don't mind giving it. If you have $40,000 in your pocket, you won't give a damn about giving a chick a few stacks. You run across a few cheap ones, but a lot of these dudes would rather spend money than time. And if they have girlfriends or wives, the payment is like an unspoken form of buying your silence. Again, some men will stick their dicks in anything with a hole, but a lot of rich men have an image to obtain. You think they gon' wife the chick with the busted weave, bad shape, and the raggedy nails? They might have sex with her, but they'd never wife her unless they molded her into the woman they wanted her to be for real. Most dudes will wife the woman that will make other men envy him, so being a bad bitch is an investment that pays off, it's also a full-time job, and we have to keep up appearances. That's where the bags, clothes, and shoes come in.

    Just the month before, a big time producer paid Mona $25,000 to get an abortion. Women everywhere go through shit with men. It doesn't matter his net worth or his profession, most men aren't shit. So, ask me if I want to deal with a broke man's shit or a rich man's shit? I still wasn't ready to make it look like I'd moved on in the public eye but behind closed doors, I needed that bag.

"Hey boo," I answered the phone in a chipper voice forgetting all about the run in with my mother.

"Hey girl. Listen, I know you trying to make this five stacks, so I'm not even gon' ask you. I'm just gon' tell you what you have to do."

"What, girl?" I asked anxiously. Just like I said, Mona keeps me plugged in.

"Nigga named Ivory, he's a big time drug dealer. I'm talking he supplies weight to half the south. You know he couldn't even get conversation out of me if he wasn't holding. Last year, he took me to Dubai. Anyway, he wants to have a threesome, and he's giving us five stacks each. He lives in Raleigh, but he's going to be in Charlotte for the weekend. What's up?"

"When does he want to do it?" my mind was going a mile a minute. I needed to get a Brazilian wax and get that damn fill-in and a pedicure. I had never had a threesome before, but who didn't need five stacks? Plus, Papi was the only dick I'd gotten since Big Draco's death. A threesome sounded like fun. I'm not into girls, but I'll be gay for the pay.

"Tonight, after he leaves the club, so probably around four."

I glanced at the time. It was four pm which would give me twelve hours to get right. "Bet. I'm about to go get my nails done and a pedicure. If my wax lady can't fit me in, I'll just touch myself up at the crib with a razor. Text me the details. I'm in."

"My bitch." Mona knew I was down, and I appreciated her for putting me on to the money. She hangs with plenty bad bitches, and she could have turned any of them on to the money.

After my nails and toes were done, I got my pussy

waxed and stopped and got take-out from a Hibachi restaurant. By the time I got home, I ate, took a shower, and climbed in my bed butt ass naked because I knew it would be a long night. I woke up at eleven and saw that I had mad missed calls. I responded back to Mona, and she said that Ivory wanted us to come to the club. I was cool with that, and I ate the rest of my food, so I could get my stomach ready for all the liquor I was about to consume. After I ate, I threw back a shot and proceeded to get dressed.

An hour later, I was walking out to my car tipsy as hell wearing a red bandage dress that looked painted on, and my long ass deep curly weave was up in a bun. On the way to the club, I made some snaps singing along to a Big Draco song, and when I arrived at the club, I texted Mona. She was already there, so I got out of my car and we met up at the door.

"My boo," she squealed as she opened her arms wide and hugged me.

Mona is gorgeous. She's half Korean and black, and she has the prettiest cinnamon colored skin. She mostly wears her long jet-black hair curly, and she's 5'3 with a body to die for. I never asked her if she had surgery 'cus it doesn't matter. I hugged her back as I peeped men watching us out of my peripheral vision. I'm used to men and women gawking at me when I'm all dressed up, and I know Mona is too. I'm that extra kind of bitch that will put on make-up and big ass shades just for a Starbucks or a Target run. Rarely will you ever see me looking busted. The very time I walk out of the house looking homeless is when I'll see a get money nigga. On this night, Mona was dressed to kill in a skimpy black dress. The entire back was out. The material in the back of the dress started at the dip in her back and barely covered her large ass. In the front, the dress had a thin strip of fabric that didn't do a great job at covering her nipples. The rest of her C cup breasts were on display for everyone to see. Her flat stomach was also exposed. The only parts of her body that were really covered were her ass and her vagina. Her pricy perfume overpowered the air around us. She smelled like money.

"You look amazing," I stated as we headed for the entrance.

Mona's fingers were tapping away at her phone. "Thank you, bae. I know Ivory wants to look like that nigga with a section full of bad bitches. I had to bring it," she looked up from her phone screen and winked at me causing me to smile.

She got a text and looked towards the door. "There he is," she stated discreetly, and I followed her gaze.

My eyes zeroed in on the man that must be Ivory, and he looked aight. He was no Big Draco or even Papi, but he wasn't what I would call ugly. Just average. His attire was very fashionable, and he had on a lot of jewelry. I wasn't close enough to see if it was real, but I was close enough to get the picture. He was holding. Not that I had to see it to believe it. Mona doesn't waste her time with broke men and to her, broke is a man that can only buy her a Louis Vuitton purse but not a Chanel bag, some matching shoes, and put a few stacks in the purse. A wide grin stretched across his face as Mona caught his eye. He walked towards us with a lil' cocky bop like he just knew he was that dude.

"Damn girl," he licked his lips as he lusted over Mona. "You not even playing fair tonight. Got damn."

"You like?" she did a lil' spin before stepping into his arms for a hug. "This is my girl, Suzon. We call her

Sue."
      With his arms still wrapped around Mona, he glanced over at me and licked his lips once again. "I know her. Well, I don't know her, but I've seen her on social media. You used to fuck with Big Draco, right?"
      I nodded proudly. This guy wasn't in the industry, and I wasn't sure if he would run his mouth, but I hoped he wouldn't. It wouldn't be a good look for me to be involved in a threesome with Mona and another dude, but I quickly remembered who she was. Mona didn't play that shit. She didn't deal with mouthy niggas. There were times she fell out with females and they ran and told her business. That shit might hit the blogs for a day or two then die down. No one really knew anything about her for real. Just speculation. Ivory walked in between us, and we headed inside the club. We made our way through the crowd and found his booth. There were already three other guys present, and they were ogling me and Mona as if we were something good to eat, and they were starving.
      They looked plenty, but no one said anything to us. Maybe Ivory had already let them know that me and Mona were off limits. I might do some things for money, but I did have some standards, and I would never have sex with more than one man in a day. If I was going to engage in a threesome with Ivory and Mona, then his friends were off limits. The drinks were flowing in abundance, and a guilty pain shot through my heart as one of Big Draco's songs came on. I felt bad for a second, then I thought about the post I had seen while I was in the nail shop. Some chick posted a video on her page for the anniversary of his death, and it had been shared a bunch of times. It was a video of them riding in a car together, and he had asked her for a kiss. I knew from

the chain that he had on that the video was made in the weeks leading up to his death. A month before he died, he spent $175,000 on a custom chain, and he had it on in their video. The shit didn't even really hurt me because he was dead, and it made me feel less guilty about what I was out here doing. If I had been the one that died, you think he wouldn't be fucking? The nigga fucked while I was alive.

Mona and I danced on each other and put on a show for Ivory which he seemed to appreciate. After an hour, I was drunk as hell and decided that I needed to slow down for a bit. I didn't need to be incoherent by the time we got to the hotel. Plus, I still had to drive there, so I needed to sober up a bit.

"Come with me to the bathroom," Mona urged.

I followed behind her, and it took every ounce of concentration that I had to keep it cute and sexy in my heels and not stagger with my drunk ass. Inside the bathroom, I got the sudden urge to pee myself, and I walked into the stall right beside Mona. I was just about to flush the toilet when I heard her sniff, and I knew what she was in there doing. I didn't judge though. I washed my hands and checked my appearance in the mirror. Mona came out of the bathroom with glassy eyes, and she sniffed again.

"You having fun, boo?" she slurred.

"I am. My ass is drunkkkk," I giggled at nothing, and that made Mona laugh too.

We partied for another hour before Ivory was ready to go. By that time, I was sober enough that I followed Mona as she followed him to his hotel. In the elevator, my heart started to beat a little fast because I wasn't sure what I was in for. Ivory got started in the elevator. He was rubbing on Mona's ass, and she was grinding on him. While he was feeling on her, he locked eyes with me and blew me a kiss. I didn't really find that sexy, but I played along and bit my bottom lip as if I was turned on. The doors slid open, and Ivory led the way off the elevator. His suite was nice as hell, and I immediately headed over to the mini bar to grab a bottle of liquor, while he sat down on the bed and rolled a blunt. I needed to loosen up just a bit more. I had never eaten a girl out, kissed one or anything, so what was I supposed to do? If this nigga was paying ten bands, I know he wanted to have a good ass time. My pussy is good. That I'm very sure of, but my freak level might only be about an eight compared to what some other females will do.

I will only have a threesome with a nigga and a female. I will never let more than one man run a train on me. I don't do anal, and I'm not sucking a nigga's toes or licking his ass. The chicks out there doing all that deserve a big bag, 'cus Suzon is not with the shit. I'll go get a job before I'm out here doing all that. Ivory was quiet while he rolled the blunt but after he lit it and took a pull, his eyes darted between me and Mona.

"Y'all get this shit lit." He stood up, walked over to a small duffel bag, unzipped it, and pulled out two stacks of cash.

That made Mona's eyes light up, and she stood up and began to undress, so I did the same. I shot her a nervous glance, and she took the lead. Walking over to me, Mona cupped my breast in her hand and ran her tongue over my nipple causing a chill to run down my spine. That shit felt great. It was no different from a man doing it. In fact, unless I was tripping, it felt a little better than a man doing it. Her mouth was wet as hell, and a moan escaped my lips as she sucked on my breast and tugged softly on my nipple. She pulled back, and her mouth found my face. Mona kissed me hungrily and passionately like we did this shit on a regular basis, and she had my pussy throbbing. Shorty was a jack of all trades because I'd never come close to being intimate with a woman, and she had my pussy leaking in less than five minutes.

"I got something you can put your mouth on." Ivory walked over to us and interrupted our kiss.

With my chest heaving up and down, I glanced down at his dick, and I almost raised one eyebrow and asked him if he was kidding me. *That's* why he was willing to pay ten bands to fuck me and Mona. His dick was average as hell. Borderline small. Don't get me wrong, a lot of niggas trick. Even ones with big dicks, but he was a regular dude with money, and I'm sure he could have gotten plenty of females to have sex with him for free or much cheaper. I know he had to be a big deal in his hometown, but he needed his ego stroked, and he felt like a threesome with females that fucked famous niggas would do it.

Oh well, if I didn't enjoy anything else, I knew I would enjoy Mona. This was just a job to me. The two of us got down on our knees and sucked him off like he had the longest thickest pipe in the world, and the moans that escaped his throat were damn near comical. We had his ass in heaven. "Got damn. Do that shit. Fuckkkkkk. Fuck yes, do that shit," he coached us as I deep throated him, and Mona sucked his balls.

I hummed on his dick and acted as if it was the best tasting thing I'd ever had in my mouth. After a few minutes, he couldn't take anymore. I followed Mona's lead, and she instructed me to lay down. I saw the two of them take a small break to snort some coke, and then he put a condom on. Mona buried her face between my legs, and he fucked her from behind. I knew her moans were more than likely embellished but baby mine were real as hell. The way her tongue swirled over my clit as she slid one finger in and out of me, I was arching my back and fucking her face like a mad woman. Mona was hands down giving me the best head that I ever had in my life. I pulled my legs all the way back and gave her all the access she needed to my pussy while I wondered how many times she'd done this. She started sucking on my clit, and I lost it. I came so loud and hard in her mouth that she giggled in my pussy. Moan came up for another sloppy tongue kiss, and I had to wonder what she was doing to me. I still wouldn't consider myself gay, but I'd have sex with her ass again for sure.

    We switched positions again, and I rode his dick while she rode his face. She had my pussy so sloppy wet that I barely felt him inside of me. No lie, he had the smallest penis I had ever had in my life, but I let out a moan here and there to appease him. We switched positions for the next hour or so. The coke and the liquor had him harder than steel for quite a while, but Mona kept me going. She was the reason that by the time Ivory came, I'd already had three orgasms. When we were done, he collapsed on the bed. I went in the bathroom and cleaned myself off. I would shower at home. I was exhausted and ready to lay down. I got my money from Mona and scurried my ass down to my car. I had a pretty good time, and I got paid well for it, so I couldn't even be mad. As soon as I started my car, a Big Draco song was on. And not just any song. A song that I always felt he wrote for and about me.

Shorty go get her own checks, come home, roll my L's, cook my food, and give me that sloppy wet sex, I never been in love, that shit wasn't meant for thugs but any time I'm down, shorty hold me up.

I had to change the station. I couldn't listen to him talk about how much he loved me, and I had just engaged in a threesome for money. Sometimes, I felt like I was losing myself out here, but what was I supposed to do? Going back to the trenches wasn't an option for me.

Natisha Raynor

ESAI 🏀

"You're newly single. I know you trying to come with us to Puerto Rico," my homie Dip said. We were in the gym working out after an intense two hour practice. Some people bitch about the fact that athletes get paid so much, but we work hard as hell and put our bodies through the most to entertain the masses.

It had been three days since I put Afrika out of my house, and my mood had been shit. It didn't make it any better that I damn near fucked up our winning streak. I was playing so bad that coach took me out of the game in the second quarter, and that has never happened. I knew I needed to get it together. Letting Afrika throw me off my game was something that I couldn't do. Aside from my sister, Dip was the only other person that I told about Afrika, and that was only because I played so bad that he knew something was wrong.

"Aggghhhh," I put the weight that I was bench pressing in its' holder and sat up. I wasn't in the mood to go anywhere and be around people. All I wanted to do was work on my game and sit in the house and sulk. "I'll pass." I picked up my water jug and took large gulps.

"My G you've been in a relationship for almost ten years. What she did was foul as hell, but you can't let that keep you down. Go have fun. Drink, party, and live your life. You already know I've invited some of the baddest bitches in the game. Listen, groupies get a bad rep, but I love them. Every now and then, you get the dumb one that falls in love, tries to trap you, might try to kill you but for the most part, they just want the money."

I furrowed my eyebrows and looked at him like he was crazy. "Do you hear what you just said?"

Dip looked genuinely confused. "What? You never had a girl try to kill you before?" All I could do was stare at him because he was seriously bugging. "Nigggaaa if a female never tried to kill you what is you out here doing? But yo, find a chick that's about her bag, and she won't give you any trouble. Use them for what they're good for and go on about your business."

I dropped my head and shook it. This is what life had been reduced to. It would take a very long time for me to ever trust any woman. I might never trust another woman if I'm being real, but I just can't see myself tricking with these high priced prostitutes. That had never been my thing. "So, you want me to buy pussy from these hoes?"

Dip shrugged. "You're going to spend money either way. You were paying all the bills at the crib, giving Afrika an allowance, and buying her things. Now that she's out of the picture, you'll be saving what? A good $10,000 a month or more. You bought her a Birkin bag. You can just have sex with one of these sack chasers, throw her $500 and never talk to her again. I'm telling you, it's cheaper, and they won't run their mouths. They know if they out you, it will make other niggas not want to deal with them. I'm telling you, it's the best."

I didn't even want to think about what Dip was

talking about. Even though I cheated on Afrika from time to time, all this shit that he was talking about, I never had to worry with. I didn't have to worry about paying women off or what I would do if I got horny. Shit, I was horny at the moment, and I didn't have anyone I could call. That dilemma had me frowning up my face and getting angry all over again. Afrika had really messed my life up, and I still lowkey wanted to choke her. I didn't even want to keep entertaining Dip's conversation, so I stood up.

"I'm about to go get some food. I'm starving."

"Think about what I said, Esai. It's only for two days. Me and two other team members are going. The women will be gorgeous, and what happens in Puerto Rico stays in Puerto Rico."

"I'll let you know," I stated in an unenthusiastic tone and grabbed my things.

I would be embarrassed to admit to anyone that it was the first day I had an appetite since I saw what I saw. I felt like a bitch, but I was in love with Afrika, so how was I supposed to feel? Every time I thought about her and Tyrese, all I could do was shake my head. They played the hell out of me and right under my nose too. There was no telling how long it had been going on. The way they were hugging and kissing when I saw them, there was no way that was their first time. No way in hell. Once I was in my 2021 Maserati, I slammed the door shut hard as hell.

I had only had the car for two months. I purchased it for myself for my twenty-sixth birthday. I also have a Range Rover and a Corvette. Most days, I woke up smiling. Thanking God that I was in the position that I was in but the past few days, I'd been waking up mad at the world. Now, I truly knew the meaning of money can't buy happiness because even though I got the endorsement with Nike and I was now worth $13,000,000 I couldn't celebrate if I wanted to. I just needed to know why. Why would Afrika cheat on me with my best friend and in my house? They didn't even have the respect to go and get a hotel room. It was almost as if they wanted me to catch them. Or maybe they thought I was just that stupid.

I stopped by a Jamaican spot and got two plates of food. I had been pushing my body to the limit, and I needed nourishment. I was so famished that in the car, I opened one of the containers and picked up an oxtail with my fingers. Yeah, that food was as good as demolished as soon as I got home. My house was twenty minutes away, and I mashed the gas without regard for the speed limit. I drove up my winding drive way and damn near crashed into the back of my Corvette when I saw Afrika sitting on my porch looking pitiful. I hopped out of the car almost foaming at the mouth.

"Fuck are you doing here?" I rushed up on her, and she flinched. She had better be scared. 'Cus she was bold as hell. Either bold or dumb as hell.

"I-I just wanted to explain. Esai, I'm sorry if I hurt you." Afrika had bags under her eyes, and I could tell she hadn't been sleeping, and that was good as fuck. I wanted her to be sad and suffering but for all I knew, she was only sad because she lost her provider.

"*If* you hurt me? Bitch, are you smoking dick?! You fucked my best friend in my house!"

"Esai, I'm sorry," a tear spilled over her eyelid. "I swear I am. I just... I don't know." She looked up at me regretfully, and I wanted to knock her ass out.

"You can't even come with a full apology!" I clenched my fists at my sides as my chest heaved up and down. "I have never put my hands on a female, so Afrika you need to leave before I do something that I could end up regretting." All I could hear was a voice in my ear saying, *don't let her fuck your career up.* And that's what might happen if I knocked her head off her shoulders. Afrika was testing me like hell, and I didn't appreciate it. I was going through enough, and I think I'd been handling it pretty well.

"The first time I slept with him was two y-years ago after I found out you cheated on me with that singer. I was hurt. I was beyond hurt because she wasn't like the others. You cheated on me with someone that was gorgeous and famous, and I was intimidated. She had her own money, and I was just so hurt. He was trying to tell me that you and her weren't like that, and we were drinking. One thing led to another, and I came on to him. It was me. He tried to resist at first." She looked away from me shamefully, and I only got angrier.

My chest felt tight. Two years ago. Wow! I watched as tears rolled down her almond colored cheeks. I knew she would bring up the fact that I cheated on her. I knew she would, and yes, I had cheated on her with someone famous before. The shit wasn't even worth it. The pussy was mediocre, and shorty was on the rebound from a rapper that had broken her heart. The one female that had the worst sex was the one that Afrika found out about, and I had to kiss her ass for almost a month to get back in her good graces. This entire time she had been holding a secret of her own. I was thinking she moved past my cheating, but she had fucked my man. I guess the joke was on me.

"How many times have you slept with him?" I asked in a low tone.

She replied in a barely audible voice, and I didn't

hear her. "Speak up muhfucka!" My eyes roamed over her locs that were piled up in a high ponytail. I took every inch of her in from her small B cup breasts to her clear skin and her naturally long lashes. Afrika didn't really like make-up, and she'd been growing her locs since freshman year in high school. They reached the middle of her back. She was one of those Earthy chicks. She liked designer labels, but she wasn't interested in all that make-up, weave, and getting her body done. When she would come to my games, she would always feel intimidated by the women around her that looked like runway models with their heels and make-up, and she would be dressed in jeans and a jersey with a bare face and her natural hair. I always tried to assure her that she was perfect, and I loved her the way she was. I didn't want my cheating to make her feel like she wasn't good enough or that she had to try and be something she wasn't, which is why I was working on being faithful.

"More than ten times. We kept saying we were going to stop. We really felt bad, but there was an attraction there. Esai, I am so sorry," Afrika began to cry, and I walked past her and into the house.

I slammed the door and acted as if she wasn't even outside. I would never in my life shed a tear over a female, but a nigga was heated. I was angry and sad all in one, and that was a deadly combination. In order to keep from exploding, I had to go in my gym and hit my punching bag until I couldn't feel my hands. I lost my girl and my best friend all in the same day, and I really wasn't sure how I was going to cope with the shit without doing something to land myself in prison.

"I knew you'd come!" Dip got excited as hell as I boarded the private jet that he had to take us to Puerto

Rico.

    I was in a slightly better mood because we had another game the night before and not only did we win, but I played much better and scored twenty-seven points. At the last minute, I decided to come because what did I have to lose? I gave my homies Rod and Lamar dap and found a vacant seat. Rod's ass is married with three kids, but I wasn't shocked to see him on the jet. I don't know one faithful athlete. Even the OG's that have been in the game for a minute and married for years that have somewhat calmed down, still indulge now and again. Some of even have other families and are living double lives. I just keep my head down and mind my business though. After Afrika did me how she did me, I'll never judge another man for cheating. I know I hurt her in the past, but she never once let me know she was going to forgive me but use my past indiscretions as a reason for her to cheat on me in the future. If that was gon' be the case, we should have just gone our separate ways. Now, my forever mood was fuck her.

    The flight attendant wasted no time bringing me a glass of champagne and as I drank it, I eyed the women that were on the jet laughing and having a good time of course with their phones out taking pictures. The first one I spotted was Big Draco's ex. Though I had seen her with some of the same women at the club that night, I was still shocked to see her on Dip's jet. I knew that Big Draco was no longer alive, but I hadn't heard about her being a pass around. Maybe I was just out of the loop. All of the women on the plane were beautiful but for some reason, she stood out to me. She had big juicy lips that looked sexy as hell while they were coated with gloss. When she smiled, she looked even better. She was bad for sure.

"You hit Big Draco's ex before?" I asked Rod in a low tone as I finished off the champagne.

"Nah. I don't know anybody that has hit her, but all that's about to change," he eyed her lustfully. "She bad, right?"

"Yeah, she is," I continued to eye her. If I could only choose one of the women out of the four that were on the jet, I'd choose her, but the mixed one that looked half Korean or some shit would most definitely come in second. There was one with blonde hair, and her face was okay, but she looked like she got her lip injections too big. I could tell that Big Draco's ex, had naturally plump lips. The blonde girl was also built like an ant. Her legs didn't match her surgically enhanced ass.

"This trip is going to be nothing short of amazing," Rod stated with a gleam in his eyes.

I didn't want to be a party pooper, but I just wasn't lit yet. I signaled to the flight attendant for another glass of champagne while everyone around me twerked and turned up. We were about to take off, and I peeped that Big Draco's ex was somewhat quiet and in chill mode like me. I decided to go ahead and try and get dibs on her before the other niggas did.

"What's your name?" I asked her.

"Suzon. You?"

I almost smirked, but I controlled myself. Not everyone watches sports and not everyone knows who I am, but Suzon was in the presence of some professional groupies. I'm sure her homegirls had googled every man on this jet, but I decided to appease her.

"My name is Esai."

"Esai. That's different. I like that." She acted as if she had really never heard my name before.

"You here with anybody?" I was under the

impression that every female present was fair game, but I wanted to make sure.

"Oh, no. I was invited by my friend, Mona."

The attendant brought me and Suzon more champagne, and I took a few gulps to loosen up. As I've said, I had cheated on Afrika before, but I was kind of new to this groupie shit. I just remembered Dip saying to find one that was about her bag. If it's understood to be all about sex and nothing more, that lessens the risk of drama and misunderstandings. "So, what's your going rate?" I came right out and asked, and she looked at me with confusion etched onto her pretty face.

Suzon's brows hiked up. "My going rate? For?"

I wasn't sure how to answer. The fact that she looked completely caught off guard had me second guessing what I said. Was I just supposed to offer her an amount? I wasn't experienced in paying for sex. I didn't respond, and she narrowed her eyes.

"Oh, you think I'm a prostitute? I came on the trip to have fun. I told myself if I clicked with someone and something happened then it happened because we're all grown, but I didn't come with a set price in mind." Her tone was even, and she didn't say it in a disrespectful way, but I could tell that I had kind of offended her. Suzon got up and walked off, and I decided not to take anymore advice from Dip's dumb ass.

If Suzon would have ended up sleeping with me for nothing that would have been amazing. I had probably stuck my foot in my mouth but if she didn't sleep with me, I'm sure someone on the jet would. So, I wasn't too pressed.

♥♥

Hours later, I was borderline drunk when I

stepped off the jet. The Airbnb that we were staying in was nice as hell. It was almost the size of the house that I lived in. There was a pool out back, and the house had six bedrooms and six bathrooms. The most amazing part was that Dip had hired a personal chef to come cook for us, and the fridge was fully stocked. We walked into a buffet like spread of steak, shrimp, king crab legs, lobster tails, seafood pasta, baked macaroni and cheese, rice pilaf, cabbage, and sweet potato casserole. My inebriated ass was in heaven and as soon as I put my bags in my chosen room, I was in the kitchen fixing myself a plate.

    I was also pleased to see the kitchen counter lined with bottles of Azul, Don Julio, Grey Goose, and Hennessey. Dip knew how to host a vacation that was for sure. He came into the kitchen as I was cutting into my steak. "Yo, I asked that Suzon broad what her price was, and she looked at me like I was stupid. Thanks for making me look crazy," I stated in a hushed voice, and his drunk ass simply laughed.

    "Nigga, please. She knows what it is. Some of them try to hang onto the that good girl role for as long as they can before they're on their knees gargling your balls. Trust me when I tell you, she will have sex with you, and she won't turn down any money. Don't keep offering the shit though," he shrugged passively and went on to fix his plate.

    Everyone else started to pile into the kitchen and once I was good and full, I poured a shot of Azul. Let the fun begin.

Suzon 💕

"Sue, baby, I know you're warming up to this, but you should have given him a price. We're all grown, and we know what it is. The fact that he's willing to pay out the gate and doesn't think you should sleep with him based off who he is, says something. These niggas aren't Big Draco. Chances are slim to none that they will wife you, so get your money, and don't be shy about it," Mona lectured me as we chose our rooms at the Airbnb, and I told her what Esai had asked me. "You should have told his ass $1,500."

I knew that every man wasn't Big Draco, but I had gotten used to being the girlfriend. I like sex, and I like money, but I didn't want to have to deal with mad niggas just to stay afloat. Why couldn't one nigga just cuff me like he had and act right? Papi for sure couldn't cuff me, but I didn't want to just be out every weekend having sex with a different man for money. When Mona told me one of her friends, Lisha wanted to come but she couldn't because she was having a herpes outbreak, I damn near threw up. She got the shit a year ago from a very famous rapper, and she was still out here sleeping around. What we're doing is really dangerous because men having money doesn't exclude them from getting diseases. Even with Big Draco, I knew he was the only one I was sleeping with, but I got checked every three months because I knew the kind of life that he lived, and these men don't always use condoms. I know some real pretty females with amazing bodies and all the designer a girl could want with bad vaginal odor because they stay letting somebody cum up in them and it keeps their ph balance throwed off. Some of these chicks carry antibiotics like packs of gum. I kid you not.

That's not what I wanted to have to do, but Mona was right. I knew why we were here, and it wasn't so I could meet my next boyfriend. I could only hope that if I flirted with Esai some and ended up sleeping with him that he'd still be feeling generous. I had just gotten $1,400 sent to my cash app for IG promotions before I boarded the jet. As long as I could keep the bags coming, I could be okay for a while but every day, I woke up scared that my fifteen minutes of fame might be over soon. She lit a blunt and passed it to me.

"This is a no judgement zone," she stared me in the eyes and was serious as hell like she was giving me a very important pep talk. "Make these few days here count. All these niggas want is to relax and get their dicks wet. Make them leave this trip thinking about you so hard that they hit you up and offer to fly you out again. If you're lucky, you might even get flown out a few times. That's the most that will happen."

I nodded before taking a pull from the blunt. I sucked the smoke into my lungs and held it there for a minute. I tried to be about this life, but I wasn't always as bold and aggressive as the other girls were. Not wanting to deal with a broke man made me a little more confident, but I had to move carefully. I didn't want the blogs linking me to anyone that wouldn't end up being around for a while. As Big Draco's ex, I just couldn't let my reputation get out there.

Tara, the ex-fiancée of a major league baseball player came into the room, and I passed her the blunt.

She was black, but she had real light skin, and her hair was dyed blonde. I wasn't sure if she wanted to pass for white, or if she just wanted blonde hair. Shit, I wasn't judging but with her hazel contacts, you'd almost think a white girl was with us. Maybe those things helped her to fit in more when she was with the baseball player. He was black but like her, he was light as hell. Alara joined us next. She is tall as hell. Alara stands around 5'9, and she has pecan colored skin and thick thighs and a big ass. She used to play volleyball, and her body is to die for. That shit is toned and athletic, and it's all natural. Alara played volleyball for seven years. Her father owns a record label, and she's plugged in with a lot of rappers. Alara was with a rapper for four years and out of the four, they were engaged for a year. They broke up and a few months later, she was with an actor. Her and the actor were hot and heavy for about five months, and now she's single again. She was there for Dip.

By the time the blunt was gone, we headed into the kitchen giggling, and all of the men were eating and drinking. "Damn we thought y'all got lost," Dip stated with a bottle of Azul in his hand. Alara went over to him, and he poured a stream of liquor from the bottle into her mouth.

I glanced over at Esai as I headed over to fix my plate, and I saw him leaning against the counter with a cup in one hand and his phone in the other. Tara was flirting with Rod, and I knew that I should go ahead and stake my unofficial claim on Esai. I eased over to him with my plate in hand.

"I didn't mean to be weird on the jet. I just haven't really dealt with anyone since my ex passed, and I really did come just to have fun. But um, I mean if everybody else is doing it..." my voice trailed off.

Esai sipped from his cup and peered over the rim at me. "It's all good." His eyes had a reddish hue, and I knew all the drinks were catching up to him. The weed I smoked had my eyelids heavy as hell, and I was starving. Not to mention, my mouth was dry. "So, you with what I'm with?" he continued to stare at me as he drank some more.

"I'm with it," I stated and went back to my food. Everyone in the kitchen was loud as hell. Music was playing, but I just wasn't all the way lit yet.

Once I was done eating, I wasted no time pouring myself some Don Julio. I was headed upstairs to change into my swimsuit. When I tried to close the door, I saw that Esai was behind me. His eyes were redder, and it was obvious that he was drunk. "You trying to fuck with me before the pool party? He asked with a lick of his lips.

Esai was handsome as hell. He had a low cut that was full of waves, and his 6'1 frame was muscular as hell. He had colorful tattoos all over his cashew colored arms, and he had pink juicy lips and a thick beard. Just the way he was gazing lustfully at me had me aroused. I drained the rest of the Don Julio from my cup and began to undress. There was a house full of chicks that were 'bout that life. Acting shy and reserved wasn't going to get me anywhere. By the time my clothes were off, Esai had pulled his shirt over his head and removed his thick erect penis from the confinement of his boxer briefs. Thinking about what was at stake, I placed a piece of ice from my cup in my mouth, dropped to my knees, and took him into my mouth.

Esai hissed loudly as the cold sensation of my mouth met with his warm dick. I took him all the way in and stared him directly in the eyes as I gagged. A tear rolled from my eye as I went to work on his dick. I closed my eyes and sucked on Esai with everything I had in me. While I deep throated him, I envisioned the bills that I had to pay and the kind of money that I needed to maintain the lifestyle that I had been living. I turned into a porn star as I slurped on Esai's dick. His breathing became shallow, and he let out a low growl. I removed his dick from my mouth with a loud popping sound, and he cursed underneath his breath as he pulled a condom from his pocket. Once the protection was secured on his dick, he walked over to me, grabbed my arm, and turned me around. When his hand pressed into the center of my back, I took it that he wanted me to bend over, so I did.

    I put an arch in my back, and Esai pressed the head of dick into my opening. The liquor and the weed had me feeling all warm and tingly inside and giving him head had turned me on, so I was ready for him, despite the fact that foreplay was lacking on his end. He eased into me inch by inch and, and I closed my eyes and let out a soft moan. His dick was about the same size as Papi's, and it felt way better than the lil' piece that Ivory was working with. Thinking back to that night had me envisioning the way that Mona ate me out, and my pussy muscles contracted on Esai's dick. He groaned as he pumped in and out of me, and my moans got louder and louder. I wasn't worried about anyone hearing me because the music was playing downstairs. Esai gripped my waist so hard that his nails were digging into me, but I didn't mind. His deep savage strokes along with flashbacks of me and Mona had my love box sloppy wet, and both our moans combined were echoing through the room.

    I was about to cum when he pulled out of me and

turned me over. As I lay flat on my back, he slid back into my gushy honeypot with ease. I looked up into his handsome face, and he had his eyes closed. I didn't want him to open them and catch me looking, but he was handsome as hell for sure. I acted as if I didn't know his name, but I did. When Mona told me he would be there I went to his Instagram, and I went through all of his pictures. He didn't appear to be in a relationship, but a lot of these men didn't post their significant others so they could appear single to the public.

  I locked my legs around his waist as my clit swelled and throbbed, and I knew I was about to cum. Desperate for the pleasure that was to come, I wound my hips in a circular motion and matched him thrust for thrust, and that shit drove him wild. "Fuck," he moaned with his eyes still closed as he sexed me so hard that the headboard was slamming into the wall. I dug my nails into his soft skin and let out a low groan as I came. My pussy felt like it had a heartbeat, and the way it gripped his dick must have been too much for him. He moaned loud as hell and erupted into the condom. I could feel the wet spot underneath me, and I wished we hadn't done it on my bed. Esai slid out of me, and his face immediately fell.

  "Fuck," he hissed as his eyes widened with panic.

  I sat up fast as hell. "What?" He didn't have to answer me though. I could see for myself that the condom was missing the tip. The shit had broken.

  "Fuccckkk," he hissed again. "Are you on birth control?"

  Even being drunk and high I couldn't miss the hopeful gleam in his eyes, and I hated that I would have to burst his bubble. "No, but we're going out tomorrow. I can stop somewhere and get a plan B pill."

"But don't you have to take that shit like right away?" He was still frantic.

"I have seventy-two hours. I know we're going shopping tomorrow. I'll get it then." I wasn't the least bit worried. I knew females that popped Plan B's like candy, and they didn't have any kids.

Esai pulled some money from his pocket and counted out $1,000. "Please get that shit. Don't do me dirty." His voice held a pleading tone, and I scrunched up my face.

"Do you dirty? Big Draco has only bee gone a year. It would look kind of crazy for me to pop up pregnant. I don't want no parts of that shit. Trust me," I assured him.

He didn't look all the way convinced. He just handed me the money and left out of my room. He may have been a pro athlete, but I didn't want to have his baby. I was too worried about what people would think. One of the reasons Big Draco's friends and family showed me so much love is because they thought I was still mourning and not dating. If I popped up with a big belly they would for sure know that I had moved past Big Draco, and I wasn't ready for that. I needed to milk his death for just a little longer.

"Bitch, are you crazy?!" Mona screeched the next day in the Uber. The Uber driver's eyes shot up and he eyed us through the rearview mirror. "Why do you want to get a plan B?" she asked in a hushed voice. "Baby, this is your come up."

I shook my head. "I can't do shit with a baby but sit home and hope that a nigga acts right. If he doesn't cooperate, then being pregnant will stop my bag for sure. I can't be dealing with other men if I'm pregnant.

You know that shit isn't a guarantee, that's why you haven't had any of yours," I pointed out. Mona had, had quite a few abortions since I've known her.

    Mona kissed her teeth. "My case is different. You're new to this. You just came into this game with Big Draco, then that ended abruptly. I've been doing this shit for a minute. I've done more club hostings than you, I have contracts with some brands, I have my YouTube channel, and I have a roster of niggas. Between all my hustles last month, I made $35,000. Damn right a baby will slow me down, plus I don't have a motherly bone in my body. Imagine me getting all stretched out and shit to deal with a screaming kid while a nigga is somewhere having fun. It will cut out club hostings and all the niggas that I deal with. I can still make good money from social media but fuck all that. It would be worth it for you to see if you could get him for child support. He's worth millions. One chick I know with kids by a ball player gets $15,000 a month for two kids. Add in your social media shit and a few racks for child support, bitch it's lit," Mona urged.

    She usually never steered me wrong, but I wasn't so sure about this. Shit, if a child would slow her down, what made her think I wanted one? She's way more of a party girl than me but still…. I didn't want to have a child by a man that I didn't even know. I knew nothing about Esai except what I read on the internet. What if he turned out to be an asshole and he fought me on paying? I couldn't afford to pay my bills and take care of a child. It was too big of a gamble, and I wasn't willing to take that big of a risk. Even though Mona acted as if I was breaking her heart, we went to the store, and I got a plan B pill. I was going to take it in front of Esai, so he would know that I wasn't on no funny shit. I'd rather sleep with men for money than trap them with a kid. I didn't want to have a child with a man that didn't want one.

We went shopping, and the other girls balled out, but I stayed on a lil' budget. I only spent $800. Mona spent around $7,000. I wasn't on her level yet, but I was damn sure aspiring to be. We shopped for a few hours, grabbed food and drinks, and went back to the house. The guys had to get back to practice, so it was our last night in Puerto Rico. The private jet was leaving at 7 am to take us back to North Carolina. When we got back to the house, the guys were looking like they'd just gotten back from a day of shopping and sight seeing as well. I eyed all of the bags in Esai's hands, and I lowkey wished he had taken me shopping along with giving me $1,000. I mean, the money is cool, but I'm sure he had a black card or something. That way, I wouldn't have had to spend my own money.

The chef was cooking, and Dip was already passing out shot glasses of liquor. I threw a shot back and headed up the stairs. I was putting my new things in my suitcase when Esai came in my room. "Did you take that?"

"No." I turned around to face him.

The wrinkles in his forehead gave way to the fact that he was irritated. "Why not?"

"I wanted to take it in front of you, so you'd know I did it. It hasn't even been twenty-four hours, Esai." I took the packet from my purse and looked around for something to drink. I grabbed a bottle of water off the nightstand, popped the pill out of the pack, and threw it into my mouth.

I could literally feel the tension wafting off of Esai's body. "Thank you. I'm not ready for no kids," he shook his head.

"Me either," I assured him.

"Last night was good though." Since Esai no longer had to worry about me being knocked up, he was back to eye fucking me.

I smiled bashfully. "Yeah, it was."

"Round two tonight?"

"Yeah, we can do that."

He left the room, and I continued to pack up my things. When I got up in the morning, I just wanted to shower, brush my teeth, and grab my things. I didn't want to have to be looking for stuff and rushing. My stomach began to rumble, and I stopped in my tracks. I literally froze and waited to see if the feeling would subside, but it only got worse. I could hear a sloshing sound coming from my belly, and I knew whatever was going on in there wasn't nothing nice. My mouth became watery, and I hiccupped. Knowing all too well what that meant, I made it to the bathroom just in time to fall to my knees and throw the contents of my stomach up into the toilet.

"Fuckkk," I groaned after throwing up what felt like everything I'd eaten for the past few days. Tears ran down my cheeks, and my stomach kept lurching even after nothing else was coming out of my mouth.

Maybe it was because I took the shot of liquor and then took the plan B pill. Shit! Had I thrown up the pill?

ESAI 🏀

I had to admit that Puerto Rico was just the getaway that I needed. Two days of drinking, chilling with my niggas and some beautiful women, and getting some good ass pussy. I came back home in a good ass mood, and my first day back at practice went well. I had given Suzon another $1,000 after we had sex the second night, and Dip was right. That shit was cool. I didn't have to worry about seeing her or hitting her up when I came back home. I wasn't trying to impress her or get to know her. We were back to our real lives, and we weren't concerned with each other. Maybe I would just stick to dealing with a groupie a few times a month rather than trying to deal with someone on a regular basis. I didn't need anyone getting attached to me or falling in love with me, because that relationship shit was dead. Afrika ruined that for everybody.

After practice, I headed to my parents' house about forty minutes away from where I live. I had been avoiding them since my break-up with Afrika. My sister told my mom what happened, and my mom was furious. She got in my ass the times that I cheated on Afrika, and she found out about them. She told me time and time again that one day, Afrika was gon' get tired of my shit. It still pissed her off to know that Afrika chose my house and my best friend to get back at me. Even if my mom was talking shit about Afrika, I didn't want to talk about her or hear about her, but I couldn't avoid them forever.

Me and my parents were close. I was also super close with my maternal grandmother, and she lived in the six bedroom house that I bought my parents my second year in the league. It was time to face the music and show them that I was okay. Was I one hundred percent okay? Hell nah, but I wasn't about to let this break me.

I pulled up in the driveway behind their luxury vehicles. My parents had good jobs my entire childhood. In fact, the house that I grew up in was almost paid for by the time I entered the league. I paid it off for them so we could have a "family house" for out of town guests, etc. and I got them another house. My mom retired after I joined the league, but my father didn't want to. He enjoyed working, and since he had a good job as a truck driver and no mortgage to pay, the vehicles him, my mother, and my nana drove were all purchased by him. I have no problem doing for my parents, but my father is a manly man. He only misses work when he has to, and he takes pride in being able to do nice things for my mom and my sister's kids. He never asks me for anything. Most times, I have to surprise him with gifts in order to keep him from protesting.

Inside the house, I found my mother watching TV in the living room with my grandmother. They were drinking coffee and eating slices of pound cake. My mother loves to cook and with her huge kitchen and every gadget known to man, she cooks elaborate meals and bakes sweets almost every day. "Hey baby," she greeted me with a warm smile.

I hugged her and then my grandmother. My mother stood up. "Come on let me cut you a slice of cake."

I chuckled. "How you know I want cake, mama?"

"Is the sky blue? I know you want cake. The

question is what kind. I have pound cake and to go on top, I cut up strawberries and there is whip cream waiting in the fridge, or I have a strawberry cake that I put real strawberries in with vanilla icing."

I groaned playfully. "Now, you know I want both of those. I'll take the strawberry shortcake now, and I'll take two slices of the strawberry cake to go. Pops still at work?" I asked as I leaned up against the counter.

"Yes. He texted me about an hour ago and said he'll be in about eight. How are you doing? And tell me the truth."

This is the part of the visit that I wasn't looking forward to. "I'm cool mama. I mean of course, I'm pissed, and I'm hurt. I've felt all kinds of emotions. Maybe I even deserve what they did to me. I just want to forget about it and move on."

My mother handed me a saucer with a slice of cake on it. "Stop talking foolish talk. You didn't deserve that shit." I haven't heard my mother curse in years, and she only curses when she's furious. "You may have done some wrong to her in the past, but that doesn't excuse her doing what she did in your house in your bed! You sleep in that bed! That's as trifling as I've ever seen, and I'm shocked at Afrika. Shocked at that no good Tyrese too. And he has the nerve to call me ma," she stated with her nose turned up in the air.

I ignored the gnawing feeling in my stomach and forced the cake down. It was moist and good like all my mother's cakes, but I may as well have been eating cotton. This was why I hated talking about Afrika and Tyrese. I shrugged passively hoping that my mother would let the conversation go. "It is what it is. She wasn't the first female to play a dirty game, and she won't be the last. She got her things off my porch, but I still have a closet full of things that I may give to Goodwill after I see if Veronica wants anything."

My sister nor my mother were anxious to go through the closet and pick out what they wanted because they were spoiled. I pay my sister well, and I bought her house and her car, so those are two bills she doesn't have to worry about. She also has good credit, so any bag or shoes or clothes that she wants, she gets them for herself. Same for my mother. My mother isn't a very materialistic person anyway. She is very classy, but she can make some slacks and a button up from Target look like high fashion. Ask my mom if she wants a Birkin or the best air fryer on the market, and she's going to say the air fryer. She was so geeked to have an ice maker that makes crushed ice, she did a damn two step in the kitchen.

I talked with my mother and grandmother for a bit, then I headed out to my car to go home. My mood had shifted from the moment my mother spoke Afrika's name. I couldn't wait to get back to normal, but I was smart enough to know that would take some time. I'd been with Afrika since high school, and I'm a grown ass man. I grew up with her. She knew things about me that Tyrese didn't even know.

"Fuck!" I banged my hand on the steering wheel. I was tired of thinking about her ass. I wanted Afrika to be dead to me. I didn't want to hear her name, see her face, or have flashbacks of our memories together, and there were a lot of them.

My phone started going crazy with notifications, and I pulled it from the pocket of my hoodie. Most of the notifications were from Instagram, but I had some text messages and even DM's on snapchat. "What the hell?" I mumbled as I tapped the Instagram icon on my phone screen.

    I breathed hard through my nose when I saw a picture on a popular gossip page of Afrika and Tyrese out at a restaurant that had an outside patio. There was a picture of them seated at a table together and a picture of them leaving. My blood began to boil as I looked at two of the most scandalous people in the world. Afrika's locs were piled on top of her head in a messy bun and large shades covered her eyes. I'm not sure if she was trying to hide, but who in the fuck would be out in public sitting outside if they wanted to be under the radar? She looked a mess, but that didn't even make me feel better. Though the large frames hid a good portion of her face, I could tell her ass was stressed. Tyrese had a fitted cap on his head, and it was pulled as low as it would go. He also had shades on, but the two idiots were still recognized. Not only that, but someone had leaked to the gossip site the fact that the two were having an affair. Before everything went down, there were tons of pictures of me and Afrika on my IG page.

    People knew she was my girl, and they knew that Tyrese was my man. Now, I was being publicly humiliated. They were still dealing with each other! That was some shit. It was making me so angry that I couldn't slap the shit out of either of them that tears sprang to my eyes, but I refused to let one drop leave my eyes. Never would I cry over a bitch or a nigga but got damn! If I could just murder their asses and get away with it, it would make me so happy. I didn't want to have to deal with this. People were tagging me left and right, and I just logged off my page. I was tempted to deactivate it, but I didn't want it to look like they had me in the feelings to the point of running me off social media. I just had to keep reminding myself that I was worth

$13,000,000. I couldn't lose everything that I'd been working towards since I was in middle school. If Afrika was out of my life, that just meant that God had something better for me. As I drove home, I tried to tell myself every positive thing that I could. I tried my best to not let my mind run rampant with thoughts of murder but when I got home, I was still pissed. I went straight to my bar and grabbed a bottle of Azul, and I wasn't going to stop drinking until I had passed the fuck out and my problems were a thing of the past.

When I'm playing ball, I try not to worry too much about who is in the stands. I knew my mother, my father, my sister, and my niece and nephew were at the game, but I was shocked to see Mona, Alara, and Suzon sitting courtside. Well, not really shocked because games were always full of groupies. I just had never seen Suzon at a game that I could recall. We hadn't started following each other on social media, she hadn't DM'ed me, or anything of the sort. She had kind of been out of sight out of mind, but I had to admit that she was looking good as hell. And her pussy had me reminiscing. I almost got a lil' shook that she was stalking me, but I let that thought go as quickly as it came. Like I said, she hadn't even liked a picture of mine or anything. Maybe she was just having a harmless night of fun out with her homegirls.

It had been two days since the news broke on the blogs about Afrika and Tyrese, and I hadn't said one word. It was so hard to be silent when it felt like everyone and their mama was watching me, but I had to remain focused. I knew if I played bad, everyone would speculate that I was in my feelings, and that's not what I wanted. The only way for me to save face even a little bit, was to appear unbothered by the entire situation. If I didn't feed into it, the shit would die down and go away. The game started off a little rocky, but I made myself focus. I blocked everything out and took all of my frustration out on the court causing me to get eight points in the first quarter. *Just focus on the game baby.* After this game, all I wanted anyone to be talking about was how well I played. I didn't need anyone feeling sorry for me or whispering about how fucked up I was playing. Nah, they could pity someone else because I wasn't the one.

    We won the game, 131-120, and I scored 26 points. I was proud of myself for making that shit happen, but I wasn't happy. I had practice early in the am, so I couldn't get too drunk, but I needed something. As I headed off the court, I eyed Suzon. She wasn't paying me any attention. She was talking and laughing with Mona, and I decided once I hit the locker room that I would slide in her DM's. Inviting her over to my crib wasn't a problem because of the gate and my security system. I'm not ever worried about anyone coming back unannounced to be a nuisance or even to rob me. I just didn't feel like getting a hotel room and going to her place was a no no. I asked her what her plans for the night were, and she said just going to a bar with Mona and Alara. I responded that I had drinks at my place, and I told her where to meet me at.

    When I left the locker room dressed and ready to go, she was right where I asked her to be looking like a million bucks. "Just tell me what you drive, and I'll come out after you. Don't want us walking out together," she stated somewhat nervously.

    "I'm in a white corvette."

    She nodded, and I kept walking. I guess I could

appreciate the fact that she was still trying to make it look like she was holding Big Draco's memory down. That meant I didn't have to worry about her running her mouth about the two of us. I got in my car and waited for her. A minute later, she was speed walking to my shit with her head down. Lil' mama really didn't want to be seen with me. That shit was almost comical. She got in, and I sped off without saying a word. After a few minutes of silence, I felt that I might be coming off as rude. Although, a part of me didn't give a damn how I came off. Me and Suzon were just sex. Nothing more. I still decided that I could say something though.

"How have you been since the trip?"

"Busy. I've done two hostings and a few photo shoots. I have to do promo all day tomorrow and another hosting this weekend."

I nodded. We were living in some lit ass times. Females got paid to post pictures on social media all day and to party. "What kind of promo you doing?" I asked even though I really didn't care.

"This girl out of Detroit sent me a wig, so I'm going to post a video of the install and some pictures. I also have a waist trainer, some flat tummy tea, five outfits from Fashion Nova, some skincare products, and some lashes."

"Damn, that sounds like a lot of pictures. People really pay you for that?"

"Hell yeah. It's the best way to advertise. Say someone sends me a wig that they made using $400 worth of hair, and I post it and get them $2,000 in sales. They made their $400 back and $1,600 in profit. You can't beat that. Sometimes, people send me hair and shit for free and just want me to shout them out, but I pick and choose with that. Like I said, if you send me $400 worth of hair and then make thousands back off my one post, that's not really a fair exchange."

I nodded. "I can dig it. I guess that's like Nike and other brands endorsing me. If people really rock with you one thing they will do is buy whatever you tell them is hot at the moment. Get your bread."

"Thanks. I'm definitely trying to be smart with my money because I don't know how long this is gonna last. I think I'm going to school to learn how to do nails and open my own shop."

It was nice to know that she didn't have cum for brains. She knew she couldn't do this forever but then again, it didn't matter to me if she was smart or not. I knew all I needed to know about Suzon and that was the fact that her pussy is good. She hadn't run her mouth about our first encounter, and I knew I could trust her to keep fucking with her. "So, you not wanting anyone to see us together, that's 'cus what? You still got Big Draco's people thinking you single?"

"I mean, nobody has asked me if I was or wasn't. I don't even think they would care. I know he was doing his thing and cheating before he died. I just guess I don't want to be attached to this man and that man. If it's not serious then people don't need to know anything about us."

"When he was alive, did you cheat on him?" I glanced over at her. "I ask because I'm starting to see that a lot of females stay with men that cheat and act like they're over it but on the low, they're out fucking too to make themselves feel better. Y'all women are sneaky as hell."

"I never cheated on Big Draco. Ever. It might sound dumb, but I loved him so much another man wasn't on my mind. It hurts like hell to see other women posting him and shit now, but they didn't do that shit when we were together. I don't like that he probably bought them shit, and had sex with them, said the same shit to me that he said to them, but we've all been dumb before. It is what it is. I can't change what happened. I just know that I'll never be dumb for a man again. That's why if we're not serious, I don't want the shit in the media. Being posted with person after person after person is kind of embarrassing because every time you end, people want to know what happened."

"I'm sure you can imagine how I feel then, huh? My girlfriend cheated on me with my homie, and the shit is all over the blogs. That's the epitome of embarrassment. Like you said, we can't change the shit though and also like you said, that shit will never happen again."

"What you getting cheated on?"

"Yeap. I can't say I'll never be in another relationship, but it won't be before I'm fifty. I bet you that shit. I'll put my hand on a hot ass stove burner before I ever trust another woman."

"I feel you on that, but us women go through it all the time. You know how tired I get of hearing that all men cheat or who cares as long as he has money. Men don't want us to want their money, but they use it as an excuse to be able to mistreat us. If my man pays all the bills and spoils me, that gives him the right to give a piece of himself to another woman? Being in relationships is too damn stressful."

"I completely agree with that, and that's why I want no parts of one. I'm glad to see that we're on the same page. I need to stop by the store and get some condoms. I was in a relationship for nine years. I don't have any at the house."

I stopped at a gas station and purchased a box of condoms. Back at my house, me and Suzon took shots of liquor. Since I had practice the next day, I only took four, but she took about seven. She was good and fucked up by the time we got into it, and she fucked me like a straight porn star. I was way more sober than I had been in Puerto Rico, and I was more coherent. Suzon's pussy was like that. So much so, that after I came the first time, my dick remained hard, and I just put on another condom and kept going. For over an hour we had some amazing ass sex and when we were done, I hopped in the shower. When I came out of the shower, Suzon told me that her Uber was fifteen minutes away. Before I could respond, she rushed in the bathroom, and I could hear her throwing up her guts. I knew she had quite a bit to drink, but an unsettling feeling still came over me. I furrowed my brows and thought back to Puerto Rico. It had been a little less than two weeks, and I had seen her take the plan B pill. But what if that shit didn't work? The toilet flushed, and I heard water running. I didn't even wait for her to come out. I stood in the bathroom door.

"When is your period supposed to come?"

She looked up at me with a confused expression on her face but that look turned to fear real quick. "Umm let me look at my phone." Suzon brushed past me and looked around the room for her phone. After she spotted it on the dresser, she picked it up and went to an app. "In two days." She bit her bottom lip and looked as if she was in deep thought.

"Do you normally throw up after you drink? Please tell me you just haven't eaten anything. I saw you swallow that pill. You sure you didn't take it too late?" I was a damn nervous wreck, and I didn't care. If I didn't have a child with my girlfriend of nine years, I for damn sure couldn't have one with a groupie that I had only known for two weeks.

"I...um.." she shifted her weight from one leg to the other.

"What?" I asked her frantically. It wasn't the time for games.

"I wasn't thinking and before I took the pill, I took a shot of liquor that Dip handed me. About ten minutes after I took the pill, I threw up. I wasn't sure if I threw the pill up or not," she explained in a weak voice, and I threw my hands up in exasperation.

"Now is a fine fuckin' time to say that shit. Why didn't you tell me so I could get you another one?" The answer came to me, and it hit me like a ton of bricks. "Yo, you are a good ass actor. I swear to God you are. All this bullshit about Big Draco. You want to have my baby. Your gold digging ass homegirls put it in your head that this is a come up? I'm not paying you shit."

Suzon kissed her teeth and laughed angrily. "You are really a cocky self-centered son of a bitch. The fuck I want to have your baby for, and I don't even know you? Having to deal with you for some money isn't worth the fuckin' hassle. I can get my own money in a few different ways. Your money isn't the end all be all. I dealt with Big Draco for over a year, and I didn't even have his baby and you are nowhere near better than him in any form, shape, or fashion," she looked me up and down with a face full of disdain. "Tonight, I'm going to pray harder than I ever have that I'm not pregnant but if I am, I can get rid of it on my own. You won't ever hear from me again. Bitch ass nigga," she spat and stormed from the room.

I gave no fucks about her temper tantrum. I

Natisha Raynor

couldn't be for sure that she did get pregnant on purpose but one thing I was sure about, was that she couldn't have a baby by me. Despite what she said about doing it on her own, I'd drive her ass to the abortion clinic myself.

Suzon ♥

    I placed the pregnancy test on the bathroom sink with shaky hands. As nervous as I was, you would have thought I was on my way to court or something. If I was pregnant, I'd just schedule an appointment to get an abortion, and it would all be over. Simple. So, I wasn't so sure why I was such a wreck. It took me a few hours and a blunt to come down off the anger that I felt towards Esai. He was a dickhead, but I mean, it's not like I would have expected him to act any other way. I for damn sure didn't think he'd jump for joy and start planning a life with me. I've never had an abortion, but I'm sure they don't feel good. I've heard there's an option to be put to sleep or at the very least be drugged up, and I would for sure pay extra for that option. Between my nerves and my low tolerance for pain, I couldn't do that shit fully awake. Regular period cramps give me a run for my money every month.

    I washed my hands and leaned against the wall in the bathroom while I attempted to wait for two minutes, but I had to resist the urge to look at the test every other second. "You are not pregnant," I mumbled some encouraging words to myself. "That was one freak accident, and you'll be okay. Maybe you should get on birth control," I continued to talk to myself. Shit, while Esai wanted to act so high and mighty, maybe I should be getting checked for STD's. I should have never told him I'd pay for the abortion myself. I should have milked him for a few stacks at the very least. "Bastard," I mumbled as my eyes fell on the test.

My eyes widened as far as they would go as I leaned in. "No. No, no, no, no, no," I rushed out as I picked the test up and held it right in front of my face. Two pink bold lines stared me right in the face, and I was on the verge of tears. So much for having a positive attitude.

I took a deep breath and calmed myself down. I grabbed my phone and headed into the living room so I could sit down and find the number to the abortion clinic. As soon as they could give me an appointment, I was going to take care of this shit, and it was a lesson learned. I would never again take a plan B pill after drinking and if I still threw up, I'd just take another one. Better yet, I was getting on some damn birth control. Big Draco and I stopped using condoms and he used to pull out. He even had a few times where he didn't pull out, and I still didn't get pregnant. The Universe really has a funny ass sense of humor. And the best part is, had I gotten pregnant by him, I'm sure he would have been happy. He wouldn't have accused me of trying to come up, and the baby would have been spoiled from the womb. I also knew that upon his death, his mother would have made sure I was straight and his homeboys too. Why did I have to get pregnant by Esai?

I found the number and ten minutes later, I had an appointment set. The first available appointment was three days away, and I hoped it wouldn't take me long to heal because I had a hosting two days after that. I was going to make $2,500 from the hosting, and I wasn't missing that for anybody. I couldn't wait for the day that I got more followers and my popularity increased because there were influencers out there getting $15,000 a hosting, and they were simple ass baby mamas. That was their come up. Just having a baby by a nigga and having a lot of followers. It hit me. My relevance and popularity would go up if I had Esai's baby despite him wanting the child or not. Even if he didn't pay child support. I could milk that shit too. I could be the baby mama that could say my baby daddy doesn't do shit for me, and I'm out here making it on my own. But what would Big Draco's fans think? Cancel culture is real as hell. Make enough people mad and when they cancel you, there goes your popularity and your money.

"Fuck," I groaned. This was a hard ass decision. I already knew Mona would be team, baby, but I called her anyway.

"Hey chica. What's going on?"

"What's going on is Esai wasted his money on that plan B pill because I threw it up and guess who's pregnant."

Mona screamed in my ear so loud that I scrunched up my face. "You about to get that bag, sis. As soon as you announce your pregnancy the blogs are going to go crazy, and your followers are going to go up. That'll keep your social media money coming for a bit. You're going to have to do as many hostings as you can before you start showing. Plus, when yo—"

She was rambling so fast, I had to cut her off. "Mona! No ma'am. I already have an abortion scheduled. I just need you to take me."

"Suzon, are you crazy? No. Why would you do that?"

I told her about my encounter at Esai's house after the game, and she acted as if she didn't hear a word I said. "Okay, so what's the problem? He doesn't have to want the baby to be ordered to pay child support. Whether he wants to or not, the law is the law. Are you one hundred percent sure it's his because once that paternity tests says it is, then that's his ass. Now, if you aren't sure about it, don't embarrass yourself."

"I'm sure it is his, but I really don't want to have a baby, Mona."

I could see her shaking her damn head over the phone. I know she felt like it would be a come up for me, but she couldn't tell me shit with all the abortions she had. Babies were a lot of work and if he never came around, then who would help me with the child? It wasn't just about money. I wouldn't let my mother babysit a dog, and Mona for damn sure wouldn't be a person I could call when I needed help. And if I ran into a rut financially, you think Big Draco's homeboys would give me money for another man's kid? In my eyes, it wasn't worth it. What good would extra money be if I was always stuck in the house with a child? I would never have a child and mistreat it. Hiring nannies and shit weren't an option either because if I found out someone was abusing my child, I'd be in prison for murder. I didn't care what Mona said. I was getting rid of it. It wasn't worth it.

"Okay. Well, at least tell him you want some money to do it. Fuck trying to prove a point to him. This man is worth millions."

Everything is about a dollar with Mona, and it can get quite annoying. I don't always want to have to think about hitting a lick or coming up every second of every day. Sometimes, I just wanted to be. I just wanted to have fun and feel loved. Being in the studio with Big Draco, traveling with him, going to shows with him, it was fun. He would smile so hard when he went out on stage and the crowd went crazy, and I'd be off to the side smiling hard as hell right along with him. I know we all have to go one day but damn. Why did he have to go so soon? Right at the peak of his career. A number one album and then boom, he's murdered. Other females had their memories with him, but I had mine too. It wasn't always about money with him. I would get mad if I didn't travel with him and he didn't call me before he went to bed. Simple things like hearing his voice and just knowing that he was okay comforted me. We had sex like rabbits because we couldn't get enough of each other. God, I missed that man something serious. I really had to wonder if I would ever be lucky enough to find that kind of love again.

  I politely changed the subject, and Mona got the hint because she started talking about her latest excursion. Ivory was taking her to the Bahamas. Mona's life was one big adventure. Imagine, traveling several times a month on someone else's dime, partying several nights out of the week, and having enough money to live lavish and not have a care in the world. Those are the things that I wanted back in my life, but I wanted them all from one man. Having to juggle multiple men and dealing with a bunch of arrogant assholes that could switch up on me at any moment wasn't my idea of fun. Esai went from being cool to really accusing me of trying to trap him. Just the memory of the words that he had spoken to me, had my upper lip curling into a snarl. He was fine as hell, rich, and the sex was good, but I planned to never have to talk to his self-centered ass ever again.

  The day of my abortion, I woke up feeling like shit. I went from not having any symptoms of pregnancy to feeling like death. If I was having doubts about getting an abortion, the way that I felt was confirmation that I was making the right choice. As soon as my feet hit the floor, I had to throw up. Once I threw up, I weakly brushed my teeth, and that took every ounce of strength that I had. All I wanted to do was get back in bed, but my appointment was in two hours. I showered, and I could barely stand in the shower. I'm not even exaggerating. I took the quickest shower in history and it took a lot of consideration as to if I even felt like putting on lotion. I felt so bad that going up in there ashy was an option, but I moisturized my body and threw on some grey sweats and a white tee. After sticking my feet in some Chanel slides, I groaned as I took my bonnet off. Looking at my reflection in the mirror, all I could do was frown. I looked pale and ragged. What in the hell had taken place in my body overnight? If this was what pregnancy was like, I wanted no parts of the shit ever whether I was in love or not. I had been awake for less than an hour, and I wanted to cry. I couldn't imagine feeling this horrid for months. I was no longer scared and actually looking forward to my appointment.

    In the kitchen, I tried to find something that I could eat that might not make me throw up. After a few moments of contemplating, I decided on some grapes and some yogurt. I ate that, drank some orange juice and guess what? Ten minutes later, I was throwing that shit up. After brushing my teeth once again, I eased my feet out of my slides and got right back in bed, and that's where I was going to stay until it was time to leave for my appointment. With the way I felt, it didn't take me long to dose off, and I wanted to cry when my phone rang, but I knew it could be Mona. And it was.

    "I'm coming," I answered in a raspy voice and

ended the call.

"Ewwww baby, you look like shit," she giggled when I got in the car, and I rolled my eyes.

"I'm glad you think this shit is funny. I feel worse than shit. I feel like death. If this is what being pregnant is like, I'm never having kids."

"Baby, out of all the times I've been pregnant, there was only one time I didn't get sick. That damn child must have been the golden child. I didn't have an abortion until eleven weeks, and I didn't get sick one time. My last abortion was at nine weeks, and I lost five pounds from not being able to eat. That fetus was a damn vampire that drained me of all my energy the entire time that I was pregnant."

"Yeah, I'm never doing this shit again." I leaned my head against the window and closed my eyes. I just wanted to get there and get this over with.

Mona was beside me with large shades framing her face and her hair up in a messy bun dressed real cute in a sundress and looking like she was that bitch even without trying too hard. I refused to sit home for nine months miserable as hell watching everyone else live their life and have fun. This was something I would never do again. If I met a man that wanted kids, he would have to pay for a surrogate. During the ride to the clinic, I dosed off again, and I woke up to Mona cursing.

"If these bible toting freaks don't get the hell out of my way, I'm running somebody over."

I looked up and saw a crowd of about ten protesters holding up signs about not murdering babies and giving them a chance to live. I didn't give a damn what their signs said. Unless they were going to help me raise the child, their chants were going in one ear and out of the other. All I wanted at the moment was this baby out of me. Mona found a park, and we got out of the car. I felt too bad to care about anything. If there was someone in there that recognized me as being Big Draco's ex, then the blogs would have a field day, but let them have it. At this point, my iron had to be a zero. Even walking into the clinic was a chore. I almost asked for a wheelchair. I took the registration forms that the chipper nurse handed me, and I damn near rolled my eyes at her. It was nothing personal, but I was on some real hating shit. What I was feeling was a level of discomfort that I wouldn't wish on my worst enemy.

I completed the forms, and Mona told me that she was going to leave. The procedure would take at least two hours, and she didn't have to stay but when I called her to come get me, she had to come, or they wouldn't release me. I was going to be drowsy and out of it, and they didn't want me trying to drive home. After Mona left, I scrolled through my phone while I waited on them to call me to the back. Twenty minutes later, I had just started getting irritated when a short Asian woman called me back. She led me to a small room where we sat down, and she began to ask me if I had considered other options such as adoption. I really wasn't trying to be a bitch, but I didn't want to consider other options. I wanted this spawn of Satan out of me but rather than tell her that, I lied and said I had thought about it. Finally, she took me to another room and told me to get undressed, and I did so.

Despite me being eager to terminate my pregnancy, once I lay back on the table, my nerves started getting the best of me. I was shivering, but it wasn't because it was cool in the room. I was scared, and I wanted them to go ahead and get the procedure over with. The doctor, a middle-aged white woman came in the room and greeted me with a smile as a nurse prepared me for an ultrasound.

"I know you gave us the date of your last period, but we do have to do an ultrasound to make sure you are the number of weeks that we calculated you to be," the doctor informed me in a formal voice.

I wondered how many of these she did a day. She sat down on a stool, and I stared up at the ceiling. Looking at the screen wasn't something that I planned to do. This wasn't a joyous occasion. It was actually anything but that. I flinched slightly at the cold gel that she squirted onto my belly and bit my bottom lip as my eyes stayed glued to the ceiling, and I waited on her to do her thing.

"Hmmm," I heard her say right before I heard a sound fill the room. It was the heartbeat, and it was loud, fast, and strong. How could the heartbeat sound so strong this early?

Something else also concerned me. That *hmmm*. That must mean something was wrong but what? I knew there was no way in hell I was farther along than I thought I was. "Ms. Lattimore, it looks like you're pregnant with twins."

My head sprang up so fast that a sharp pain shot through my neck, and I barely even felt it. "Wh-what? There must be a mistake." My eyes shot over to the monitor even though I wasn't too sure of what I was even looking at.

The doctor pointed to a spot on the screen. "Here. One sac with two embryos which means identical twins. You can still go through with the procedure of course, but it will be $100 extra."

Tears sprang to my eyes. It would be so easy to just lie back and let her suck these things out of me, but how could I abort *two* babies? It would be double the trouble carrying them and taking care of them, but I couldn't live with getting rid of two babies. The reality of the situation hit me like a ton of bricks, and I started bawling like a baby. I was crying so hard that the nurse came over and put her arms around me. The doctor sat patiently and waited for me to get myself together.

"If you are having second thoughts or even act like this isn't what you want, then I can't do it. Do you need some time? You can even come back another day if you'd like."

"I don't need to come back another day. Thank you." I couldn't say the words but when I sat up, she knew that I wasn't going to go through with it.

She gave me a small smile, and her and the nurse left the room so I could get dressed. The tears had stopped, but I was still devastated. Just because I couldn't bring myself to abort two babies didn't mean I was happy about being pregnant with twins. I shot Mona a text message and told her that I was ready. I wasn't looking forward to a conversation with her because I knew she would be all upbeat and optimistic and shit. While I was home miserable, she would be out partying, drinking, smoking, snorting coke, and getting money. Once I had the babies, how could I go back to hosting and turning up and shit? Who was going to watch two babies while I 'worked'? My grandparents could probably watch them for an hour or two tops, but they were up there in age. Two babies would give them a run for their money. And they damn sure couldn't be up in the wee hours of the morning feeding babies. What would carrying twins do to my body? I would probably have to get surgery after I gave birth.

Those were all thoughts that were running

rampant in my mind when I walked out of the clinic and spotted Mona waiting for me. I knew when she saw me fully alert and walking on my own, she would know that I didn't go through with it. As soon as I closed the car door, she started. "I'm going to be an auntie, aren't I?"

I put my head back on the headrest. "It's twins, Mona. I couldn't live with myself if I got rid of two kids, but I feel like shit already. How am I supposed to carry two damn humans inside my body? And what am I supposed to do about money? I can't do clubs and shit with two kids sitting on my bladder."

"Two kids! Bitch, that's double the child support!"

I felt too bad to ignore Mona's ass today. I looked at her with a face full of frustration. "Everything is not about money, Mona! If Esai doesn't want these kids, which I'm sure he won't, he can drag a paternity test and child support court out for a minute. I can't pay the rent on my condo working a regular job. I'm going to be fucked. How in the hell do I go from being a popular influencer to a struggling mother of two?"

"First of all, stop being dramatic. Just calm down and let's think about this," Mona stated calmly as she pulled off. "Now, you have at least a few months before you start showing. You have to woman up and act fast. I know morning sickness will kick your ass, but you need to hurry and do some sexy photoshoots in some sexy ass lingerie. Go crazy with the pictures and get your following up even more. Also, take as many pictures as you can a day. You need to stockpile mad photos so you can post them after you start showing and no one will even know that you're pregnant. Even after you start showing, you can still do videos of your skin care routine and promote for skincare, lashes, and hair brands. You can continue to go live and only show your face. This isn't the end of the world for you, so stop acting like it is."

I still wasn't looking forward to carrying twins, but she was right. I had started to feel better already. She had come up with a solid ass plan and once my babies were born, I could milk that shit for all it was worth. By the time I had my kids and were ready to show them to the world, it would have been almost two years since Big Draco passed. At some point in time his damn fans, friends, and family would have to get over that shit because life goes the fuck on. Mona gave me a pep talk all the way to my condo and once I was inside, I fixed a bowl of soup and climbed into bed. My phone rang, and I saw that Papi was calling. I hadn't spoken to his ass since the night in New York.

"Yeah," I answered the phone dryly, and he already knew I had an attitude.

"Don't be like that. I been out of town running crazy and up until this morning, my wife was with me, so I couldn't call like that. I see you been hanging with Mona and Alana heavy. They got you out on the hoe stroll with their asses?"

If I didn't know any better, I'd say he was jealous, but we could never be for many reasons, so his jealousy was invalid. "I don't know what you're talking about. I've been having fun. What's the harm in that? You do it, right?"

"Fuck what you talking about. I'm trying to see you this weekend. You have a hosting, right?"

"Yeah. I do."

"Bet." Papi was quiet for a few seconds, and I was just about to say something when my phone dinged. I took the phone away from my ear and saw that Papi had sent me a cash app for $2,500. "You get that?"

"Yeah, I got it." I put a spoonful of soup into my mouth. "Just call me when you get in town."

"Bet."

I ended the call and sighed. I hated when Mona made everything about money, but that's exactly what I was going to have to do now. I was going to have to entertain Papi for as long as I could and get all that I could out of him. I needed to go ahead and start saving my money for these babies, and I was going to start with the money he had just given me. There would be no more designer purses and blowing money on dumb stuff. Shit was about to get real.

Natisha Raynor

ESAI

I know I'm the last person that you want to hear from, but I had to say something. You've done too much for me and been too good of a friend to me for me to not say anything. Sorry doesn't suffice. I know you hate me, and you have every right to. I threw away years of friendship being disloyal. You never switched up on me, and I will regret betraying you until the day I die. I know that nothing I say is enough. I tried so hard, bro. I tried to deny her, and I tried to stop. I even tried to flip it, and I told myself you didn't deserve her because you were cheating on her and not even that made me feel better.

  I had to stop reading before I threw my phone across the room and broke it. This nigga had some nerve. He went from apologizing to telling me that basically he fell for my girl, and he couldn't stop messing with her. Tyrese was asking for an ass whooping. There were times that I really thought about just accepting whatever came with breaking his nose. I wanted the season to be over, so I could smoke weed and get shit faced drunk like I wanted to without having to worry about practice or drug tests. I was sick of trying to play my way through this bullshit. From what my sister said, Afrika deactivated her social media because she was getting so much hate for what her and Tyrese did, and that still wasn't enough for me. Now that everyone knew I was single, females were sliding into my DM's left and right, but I wasn't even in the mood for all of that. I erased Tyrese's message and got on IG. On my explore page, I saw a picture of Suzon looking good as fuck. She was wearing a white thong and a matching bra standing in front of a nude backdrop, and she looked like pure perfection. Shorty was bad as fuck, that much I had to admit.

    I hadn't heard from her since she left my house, so I assumed that meant she wasn't pregnant, and I had to breathe a sigh of relief. Her picture had over 6,000 likes, and I had to admit that she was doing her thing on social media. I put my phone down long enough to walk over to my bar and pour myself a double shot, then I went right back to it. I made my way through Suzon's pictures, and I started thinking about what that mouth did. Her pussy was wet as hell, and it felt like heaven with a condom. I wondered what that shit would feel like if I slid up in there raw. I finished off my drink and despite the intensity of our last conversation, I slid in her DM's. More in an effort to make conversation than me actually being worried.

    Did your period ever come?

    The question was simple enough. While I waited on her to respond, I decided to flirt with some of the women that had taken it upon themselves to hit me up on social media. One of them had light skin and curly blonde hair, and she reminded of the rapper, Mulatto. It's an exhilarating feeling when some of the baddest women in the world throw themselves at you, and you don't even have to work for the pussy. I saw that the chick with the blonde hair lived in LA. That was cool and all, but I needed something local. I was finally a bachelor, and I could do me without sneaking. I had been sleeping. I should have been up in something new every night of the week while I was home feeling sorry for myself. ZaZa and I flirted for about twenty minutes before I realized that Suzon hadn't messaged me back. Her ass lives on social media, so I doubted she didn't know that I had hit her up. Sure enough, when I went to the message, it said *seen*.

 Being that she wanted nothing to do with me, I could only assume that her period had in fact come, and that she was just being a bitch. I wanted to believe that, but I had this nagging feeling. If she wasn't pregnant, why not just tell me that? I'd give her whatever if she'd just have an abortion. The longer she went without responding to me the more worried I became. I couldn't even concentrate on flirting with ZaZa. I didn't have Suzon's number or anything. I could try and get it from Mona, or I could just let that shit be. I wanted to say fuck her so bad, but I didn't want her popping up five months from now with a big ass belly when it was too late to get an abortion and demanding money from me. I just needed confirmation that she wasn't pregnant, and she could go on about her business as if she never knew me.

♥♥

 Suzon wouldn't respond to my message, so I decided to pop up at the club she was doing a hosting at. I had a game that night, and it was our first loss of the season. I went out with Bakari and Dip and by the time the game ended, and we were showered and ready to go, we pulled up at the club right at midnight. It was becoming packed but because we were who we were, we were led straight to a VIP section and as luck would have it, we ended up in a section right beside Suzon. I walked by and locked eyes with her, and she frowned her face up at me slightly. I could only smirk because she was fine as hell when she was mad. I gave her a quick once over, and she was dressed in a black corset top and black short shorts with snakeskin print thigh high boots on. Her weave was hanging down to her ass, and she had on tons of make-up. I spotted Alana and Tara in her section. They were turning up and having a good time, but Suzon was sitting down with a bottle of water in her hand.

    I decided to let her live and not say anything to her right away. I was just going to observe for a minute. Dip and Bakari busied themselves with inviting women to our section, and a tall dark-skinned female took to me right away. She was fine as hell and if all went well, I'd be having sex with her in the next few hours. The drinks were flowing in abundance, and the club was hype. I was having a good time despite us not winning our game. Shit, no matter how much we want to, we can't win them all. Every now and then, my eyes would dart over to Suzon, and she was turning up, but she didn't seem like her usual party going self. She wasn't as turned up as her friends, and she was still sipping water. I tuned out everything Jordyn was saying to me as I watched Suzon sip her bland beverage. Water in the club? I'd seen females drink water when they were on ecstasy or molly, but I had a feeling it was more than that. My palms grew sweaty, and I needed to talk to her ass ASAP. I also had to remind myself to be very diplomatic. I wouldn't get anywhere by pissing her off. Once she was offended and defensive, she would go against what I wanted out of spite, and I couldn't risk that. She claimed that she didn't want anyone to know about us and that she didn't want to have my kid, but I didn't quite believe that. All she had to do was tell me her period came, but she couldn't even do that. Maybe because it hadn't come.

I waited and let the DJ shout her out and waited for some of the eyes to be off her. As discreetly as I could, I made my way into her section, and I stood directly in front of her face. Suzon refused to make eye contact with me. "Look, the last thing we need to do is make a scene in the club. I want to make this as quick as possible before rumors get started. I'm sorry for how I came at you at my house, I just got scared. Can you answer my question, please? All I want to know is if your period came. I have a right to know."

Suzon finally looked at me, and I could tell that she was still pissed at me but the longer she stared at me, the softer her face became. "Like you said, we don't need a scene in the club, and we don't need rumors started, so I'll say this quickly. It didn't come. I went to get an abortion, and the doctor told me that it was twins, and I couldn't get rid of them."

My heart pounded heavily in my chest as I stared at her and waited for the slightest sign that she was lying. Maybe she just wanted to piss me off, but I took in the bottle of water in her hand. She wasn't lying. All I could do was turn and walk away. I wasn't sure what I had done to make God mad, but I was paying for my sins something serious. First, my girl cheated on me with my best friend and now, I was having twins with a woman that I barely knew. I didn't even know Suzon's last fucking name.

"You good?" Bakari asked as I came back into the section.

I had become a master at hiding my emotions, and it wasn't the time to drop the ball on that. I couldn't tell anybody about this. "Yeah, I'm good, bro."

I was anything but good. As I picked up a bottle

of tequila and poured myself a shot, all I could do was think about what a shit show my life had become. Karma for cheating on Afrika so many times maybe. I could block Suzon and try to go on with my life but once those babies were born, she was bound to tell people that I was the father. Even if I chose not to be in their lives, I'd still have to pay if they were determined to be mine. On top of that, my parents would never ever walk this Earth and know that I had kids out there and not be in their lives. What kind of man would I be if I denied these kids and didn't take care of them? Life was shitting on me heavy, and I was tired of it. If I offered her money to get rid of them, she would probably turn me down because let's be real, she would get anything I offered her back in child support.

I threw my shot back and leaned over so that Bakari could hear me. "I'm 'bout to be out man. I got a fine lil' thing waiting on me," I lied. I couldn't do it anymore. It felt like I was suffocating in that damn club.

Bakari gave me a wide grin and extended his hand to give me dap. "That's what I'm talking about my guy. Have fun and be safe."

"Already," I tipped my head in his direction and said my good-byes to Dip.

This shit was getting out of hand. People tried to stop me and speak to me as I headed for valet, but I only had tunnel vision. That shit was dangerous because I'm a millionaire and wasn't being focused on my surroundings. I never worry about getting robbed or anything like that when I go out, but I know it can happen. People recognize me everywhere that I go. The way I was feeling, if I did get robbed, I probably wouldn't even care. For the past few years, life had been pretty good. Too good I guess because now, I was being hit with shit left and right. I don't have any childhood horror stories. My parents weren't abusive or toxic. They argued like any other couple, but it never got to a point where it affected me or my sister negatively. We weren't abused, we didn't live in poverty, the only time I got mad at my father was when I felt he pushed me too hard in basketball, and that had paid off in the end. I was raised the right way, and it wouldn't sit well in my spirit to be a deadbeat to not one but two kids but got damn! I didn't want kids right now, and I damn sure didn't want kids with Suzon. She was fine as hell but in a I want to get my dick wet kind of way. Shorty poses for pictures in her bra and panties to post on social media. I'm not exactly against it, but I couldn't be with a woman like that. No telling how many niggas in the industry she'd been with, and I was supposed to be proud to have her as my baby mama. Yeah right.

    The valet driver brought my car around, and I tipped him, got in, and drove off. I had a few ways I could approach this situation. I could act as if Suzon didn't exist and wait until the babies were born to have a paternity test. If they were mine, maybe we could settle on an amount for me to give her every month and hopefully, she wouldn't give me shit. I know she claimed she could do it on her own, but how long can social media fame really last? A lot of these women have all these designer bags and clothes, and they don't have a pot to piss in in real life. For all I knew, she could have my babies and take them to some shitty neighborhood to live in. I clenched my steering wheel tight and pulled my lips into my mouth. Frustrated wasn't even the word to describe how I felt. I had fucked up big time listening to Dip. *Just fuck with groupies.* It may have worked out for him, but that shit had been a dud for me so far.

Another way to handle the situation would be to get a blood test done while she was pregnant and if the babies were mine, I would be there for her during the pregnancy. I'm a big believer in karma, and I really felt like if I shitted on my kids, God would make me suffer for that. I don't know one deadbeat father that prospers in life. At the end of the day, even if I was to shoot her $1,000,000 it wouldn't come close to breaking me. After my employees and the expenses for my commercial cleaning company are paid, I profit around $5,300 a month. Which isn't really a lot, but I don't touch that money. It's been sitting for years, and I have over $100,000 just from that. I can very well afford two kids, but I just wasn't ready to be a father. There is more to being a father than money. I now would have to deal with a woman that I barely knew for the next eighteen years. I wanted to just keep driving and driving until I ended up on the other side of the world, but that wouldn't solve shit. With all of the shit going on in my personal life, I didn't know how I was going to keep playing well this season. We had five more games left, and I was lowkey ready for them to be over. My head and my heart weren't even in basketball for the first time in my life, and I didn't like that feeling. It was my contract year, and I had to play my best. When it was time to renegotiate, I was going to try and go for $10,000,000. Shit, I would now need that money more than ever.

Suzon ♥

"This pussy so tight and juicy," Papi moaned in my ear.

He just didn't know how bad I wanted him off of me. My morning sickness hadn't gotten any better and the day of my hosting, I stayed in bed all day drinking green smoothies and eating soup in an effort to try and rest and get myself together. I only had to be at the club for four hours but when you feel like you're dying, four hours is a long time. As soon as I left, Papi hit me up, and I had to fuck him. I knew he hadn't given me that $2,500 for nothing. I clenched my pussy muscles on his dick and moaned for him. I just wanted him to cum, so he could leave, and I could go to sleep.

"Papi," I moved my body underneath him fucking him back, and he snaked his tongue into my mouth.

Papi groaned into my mouth as he slammed in and out of me, and I started to feel like I had to throw up. Just as I was about to tell him to stop, he let out a loud ass moan as he erupted into the condom. "Fuck girl. You got some good shit," he panted as he rolled off of me.

I closed my eyes briefly as he went into the bathroom. I was really trying to concentrate on not throwing up. Every time I thought about enduring nine months of this shit, I wanted to cry. I had to get some candy for nausea to suck on while I was at my hosting. It was by the grace of God that I made it, and I had another one coming up in a week, in Greensboro, North Carolina. I would have to brave through it because I needed all the money I could get. I had taken Mona's advice and done the sexy photoshoot. My hair, make-up, and actual shoot had taken a total of six hours and by the time I left, I barely had the energy to drive home. I've never felt this bad in my life. I had to really thank God, that I didn't have to rely on a traditional 9-5. I planned to sleep the day away, then wake up, do my hair, and take pictures of the promo products I'd been sent and get right back in bed.

Papi came out of the bathroom and smirked at me. I guess he thought he had put it on me so good that I couldn't move. He didn't even know the half. "I heard that ball player nigga was in your section tonight. Esai."

I peered at Papi with an annoyed expression on my face. Normally, after sex he just straight up left. I was never sure if it was because he felt guilty or not but normally, he'd be on his way out the door by now. I wasn't interested in conversation. "Okay, and? What does that mean? People be talking about and worried about the wrong shit."

"You looking for somebody else to fuck with? Tired of being single?"

I sat up in bed. "Papi, I'm not even understanding why you're questioning me so hard. You're married. Why does what I do concern you? We don't even talk on a regular basis. We see each other like once a month, fuck, and then you're out without even saying good-bye."

He glared at me for a moment. He put his clothes and shoes on without speaking. After he grabbed his keys off my dresser, he tossed another look my way. "Don't let me find out you talking to none of these niggas, Suzon." He came over and kissed me on the lips roughly then left the room.

    I just stared after him trying to figure out what in the hell that was about. He picked the wrong time to try and be jealous. Seeing as how there were two babies in my body, I wasn't sure when I would start showing. I know most times it takes around four months with one baby. I would be lucky to make it that long. That's why I couldn't bullshit with taking my pictures and getting in all the promo I can in tight ass clothes that I can barely breathe in when I'm not pregnant. Even if I can hide my pregnancy from social media, I won't be able to hide it from Papi forever. I don't have feelings for him, and he's married. I don't care about losing him. I do however, care about losing his money.

♥♥

    I slept until two pm, got up to pee, ate some scrambled eggs on toast, and threw the shit up. I was so frustrated that I cried. I couldn't keep feeling like this. I absolutely hated it. I got back in bed and bawled like a baby. After I got myself together, I got on social media and saw that I had a message from Esai. My heartrate increased as I opened it up to see what he wanted. If he was going to try to force me to get an abortion or if he was talking shit, I was just going to block him.

    We need to talk. Since we can't do a public place, can I come to you?

    I looked at the time and saw that he'd sent the messages three hours ago. I responded back with my address. I could keep my attitude and attempt to play tough, or I could hear Esai out and hope that he would help me with these damn kids. I couldn't change whether or not he thought I trapped him, but if he wanted to help, he damn sure could. If he didn't want anything to do with the kids, I would do it alone, but his help would be greatly appreciated. I wasn't in the mood to kiss his ass, but I also didn't want to make things harder on myself than they had to be. I was already sick as a fuckin' dog.

    A big part of me didn't care about what Esai thought about me, but I just couldn't have him come over with me looking like absolute shit. I took my bonnet off and redid my ponytail so that it was fresh and neat. I cleaned my face and put on moisturizer. I brushed my teeth and gargled with mouthwash before placing clear gloss on my lips. I showered, put on lotion and dressed in a simple pair of black leggings and a black sports bra. That's the best it was going to get. I took the rest of the energy that I had and made my bed and cleaned my room. I lit candles and curled up on the couch with my favorite throw blanket, popped some of the candy for morning sickness into my mouth, and found something to watch on TV. A few hours passed, and I had dosed off when my doorbell rang. I jumped up startled, and my heart was beating wildly in my chest. That always happens when my phone or doorbell rings when I'm asleep, and I hate it. In an effort to calm my nerves, I placed one hand on my chest and inhaled a deep breath. It hit me that Esai was at my door, and that didn't help my nervousness at all. I threw the blanket off my legs, got up, and stepped barefoot to the door.

    When I opened it, Esai stood in the hallway looking just as unsure as I felt. I stepped back so he could come in, and he crossed the threshold of my condo. I noticed he was looking around. I'm sure he wanted to check out how I lived, and it was whatever. I wanted Esai to know that I wasn't some pauper that needed him to survive. True, I'm always looking for a come up but if need be, I can make shit happen myself.

This social media shit isn't as easy as it looks. People think it's easy money and in a way it is, but there's always the need to look, act, and be perfect. As soon as another woman comes along with a pretty face, amazing body, and cheaper prices, then your ass is on the back burner. I don't always want to have to sit still for an hour or more getting my make-up slayed four times a week or watching what I eat all the time and working out, unless I want to keep going to get surgery. The feeling that you have to look nothing short of amazing all the time is draining, but that's what we get paid for. People want their clothes on perfect bodies. They want their lashes on pretty popular faces. They only pay the top tier bitches for promotion. Sometimes, I just want to hide out in my condo and be ugly for a few days and pig out on food, but bills don't get paid like that.

    I headed over to my couch, and Esai was right behind me. We sat in an awkward silence for a few moments, and I decided to speak up. "Look, I know you think that this pregnancy is some kind of a come up for me, but I can show you the ultrasound from the abortion clinic. I was there. When I found out it was two babies my conscience wouldn't let me get an abortion but make no mistake about it, this isn't a happy time for me." I didn't expect to become emotional, but my voice cracked, and tears filled my eyes. "For the past few days, I have felt like crap. I throw everything up. I have zero energy. I produce mad saliva. My breasts hurt, and did I mention I feel like absolute shit. I hate everything about being pregnant. You get to still go out, live your life, and deny these kids for as long as you want. My life is forever changed. Not yours."

    "How is my life not forever changed? You're not the only one with a conscience. I thought real hard about walking away and not looking back, but I wasn't raised like that. It's not my fault the condom broke, and it's not your fault you threw the plan B pill up. For whatever reason, these babies are supposed to be here, and it is what it is. If you're at least nine weeks pregnant, we can get a paternity test done. If the kids are mine, we can come up with a number. I'll do my part."

He didn't act exactly thrilled, but at least he was offering to help. That's all I could really ask for. I didn't expect him to be happy. Shit, I wasn't happy my damn self. "I'm seven weeks. I'll let you know when I'm nine, and you can make the necessary arrangements. I'll give you my number unless you want to keep DM'ing me."

Esai pulled his phone from his pocket, and I called my number out to him. He called my phone, so I would have his number. "Is there anything you need?" he peered up at me, and I could tell he was sad. Maybe defeated. Stressed. This wasn't ideal for me either, and I appreciated him not barging up in my crib on some arrogant macho shit throwing his money around and demanding that I get rid of these kids. Because then, he would have gotten cursed out and blocked for real. And I just might have gone to the blogs just to be spiteful.

"No. Unless you know where I can buy some energy," I half-joked. "I've just pretty much been sleeping and waiting to feel better. I have to do my hostings and promotions because those pay the bills. Other than that, my bed and this couch are my best friend."

"I'll see how things are going in a few days." Esai stood up, and I stood up as well.

I walked him to the door, and he left without saying good-bye. I wasn't as hype about this shit as Mona was. Honestly, I would have rather continued to get money how I was getting it. Despite feeling like shit, I was hungry, so I headed to the kitchen to make a smoothie. Sometimes, those stayed down better than food. I added ice, almond milk, grapes, apples, oranges, bananas, mangos, strawberries, and spinach. I had just taken a few sips when my phone rang. I rolled my eyes towards the ceiling when I saw that my mother was calling. I could only imagine what she wanted. I would bet money she wasn't calling to ask how I was doing. I had no desire to even tell her that I was pregnant. She would find out when she found out.

"Hello?" I answered in a dry tone.

"Suzon, Barbara from next door's apartment caught on fire and before the fire department got here, my apartment got smoke damage. My clothes and furniture are ruined, and I can't stay here. I'm on my way to your grandparents' house, but I was wondering if you could help me out with some stuff. I wouldn't ask if I didn't need it. All I have are the clothes on my back."

I rolled my eyes so hard I'm surprised they didn't get stuck. I plopped down on the couch and didn't feel at all guilty about what I was going to say. "I can send you a little something, but that's all I can do. I have my own stuff going on." I ended the call without waiting for her to respond, and I didn't give a damn how she felt.

These babies had my attitude on a hundred. She didn't get a pass just because she's my mother. I never get a call saying, *hey, I was just checking on you. Hey, I cooked do you want a plate? Hey, do you need anything?* The only calls I get are the ones where she asks me for money, and I was sick of it. I sent my mother $500 through cash app, and I made up my mind that she couldn't get anything else out of me. I didn't have room in my life for anyone's toxic, draining, blood sucking energy. In nine short months, I would be the mother of not one but two babies, and I needed to get my shit together.

Natisha Raynor

ESAI 🏀

    Two weeks after I visited Suzon's condo, I went back over because we were having the paternity test done. Money talks, and I was able to pay for the people to come out to Suzon's condo so they could draw our blood. We were both still trying to be cautious about going out in public. Even if these kids turned out to be mine, I still didn't plan on telling my friends and family for a bit. Suzon has a nice condo and a nice car. I don't doubt that she gets paid well to do what she does, but she's not rich. She might even be able to take care of these kids on her own, but my money was needed. I was hoping that I wouldn't have to battle with her about money all the time. I had already decided once the test came back to offer her $5,000 a month. That would more than cover diapers, formula, wipes, and any other baby needs for two kids. Babies didn't need designer, and if she wanted to put them in daycare, we could discuss that cost later. It was my job to take care of the kids, not her. I would never offer her twenty plus thousand dollars a month and if a judge ordered me to pay that much, I'd do everything in my power not to pay it. Most women take that kind of money and take lavish trips every month and go back to living their same pre-baby lavish life while spending the child support and half raising their own child.
    I rang the bell, and she answered dressed in black

yoga shorts, a black tank top, and brown Louis Vuitton slippers. Her hair was in long blonde faux locs, and she didn't have any make-up on. She looked pale and tired, and I could tell pregnancy was kicking her ass. She wasn't even on social media much anymore. My eyes zeroed in on her ass, and it looked bigger than the last time I saw her. Her breasts had damn near doubled in size. Her body was definitely changing even though her stomach was still flat.

With the stress of her pregnancy, I hadn't had too much time to dwell on Afrika and Tyrese's betrayal. I still wasn't the same happy go-lucky person I was before all this bullshit, and I was still drinking way too much. "How you feeling?" I asked Suzon as I closed the door behind me. I was asking more because it was the polite thing to do and not so much because I cared. It was weird as hell having a stranger pregnant.

Suzon shrugged passively. "Still the same really. Sleeping way too much. I feel unproductive as hell, but when I push myself, I end up paying for it," she grumbled, and I could tell that she hated being pregnant. "I have a hosting this weekend. I can handle one a week."

"How long you going to be doing hostings?" I inquired with furrowed brows.

"Until I start showing. I pray that I have at least three more months before that happens, but we'll see." She looked down at her stomach as if she expected it to grow before her eyes.

I could respect the fact that she was still trying to get her own money and not depending on me. The doorbell rang, and she moved to answer it. Suzon let the phlebotomist in that had come to draw our blood. A friendly white woman smiled at Suzon then me.

"Hi. I'm Elizabeth, and I'll be drawing your blood today. The process is very simple, and I won't even be here thirty minutes."

I already paid over the phone, so I simply nodded and listened to the instructions. She didn't lie when she said it was simple and easy. She drew my blood then Suzon's, packed everything up in her bag, and she left. There was always a slight tension or awkwardness in the air whenever me and Suzon were around each other. You would never know that we'd have sex four times. I've seen her naked, and she's had my dick in her mouth, yet there were times that we seemed uncomfortable around each other. I was never sure of what to say. If these were my kids though, I was going to have to get used to saying something.

"I'm gonna head out. You need anything?"

"No. I'm straight. Thanks for asking."

"Bet."

In the elevator, I retuned a missed call from Bakari. I had been dead set on keeping this shit a secret, but I needed to tell somebody. I needed some advice. Bakari is single, and he has a two-year old daughter by his ex. "Yo."

"What you got going on, nigga? Matt is having a party tonight. He rented an Airbnb. You down? I'm leaving out around eleven, if you want me to come scoop you."

Bakari actually lives two streets over from me. Going out didn't sound bad. Even though I'm usually exhausted after practice and my workouts, I was still kind of tired of sitting in my massive house alone night after night. This couldn't be life. I had been living with someone for the past three years, and it was weird as hell living alone all of a sudden. "Yeah, you can do that. I wanted to holla at you about something though. And I trust that you'll keep it to yourself." The elevator doors slid open, and I stepped off and made my way out of the building.

"You know I'm not the type to run my mouth. What's good?"

Bakari is from New York, and his accent is thick as hell. "You know that chick Suzon. The one that used to go with Big Draco?"

"Yeah. She bad as fuck."

"Yeah, well I fucked with her on Dip's trip to Puerto Rico. The condom broke, and she threw the plan B pill up. Shorty is pregnant with twins. I just left her crib getting a blood test done. I'll have the results in about three days."

"Damn bro. She bad as hell but shit. I'm going to assume you didn't want kids because you and your girl didn't have them."

"Hell nah. We never even tried. She said she went to get an abortion, and when she found out it was twins, she couldn't do it. I can honestly say that pregnancy is kicking her ass, and she doesn't enjoy it. I feel like she would rather get an abortion, but her conscience won't let her."

"Ummm I don't know bro. Some of these females are good ass actors. I know a shorty that can start crying at the drop of a hat. I'm talking real ass tears bro. I've seen chicks have thirty abortions then refuse to have one by a nigga that they feel they can come up off of. Has she asked you for any money so far?"

I pulled out of the parking space. "No. She's still doing hostings and shit. Still getting money off social media and every time I ask her if she needs anything, she says no. I'm going to see if we can settle on a set price and avoid child support court."

Bakari let out a low whistle. "Good luck with that one. My bitch ass baby mama wasn't having no parts of anything I was offering. She ran to a judge because she wanted to get the maximum amount. He ordered me to pay that hoe $6,000 a month. Two months after I started paying, that bitch was in Punta Cana with her hoe ass friends."

All I could do was shake my head. Suzon was having two damn kids, so imagine me having to give her $12,000 a month! It wouldn't break me, but who wants to give a female $12,000 a month of their hard-earned money? I'm the one in the gym seven days a week for hours on end, running, shooting, sweating, sacrificing. That shit isn't fair. Especially when the money isn't being spent on the kids.

"You think if I offer her $5,000 a month, she'll turn it down?" I was starting to become worried all over again.

"I don't know man. If she has friends that know about how much the judge will order and they get in her ear, she might act like that $5,000 isn't good enough. It just depends on what kind of a person she is. Just try to stay on her good side. Kissing ass never hurt nobody."

I was once again pissed for even being in this situation. "Fuck it. I used to give Afrika's grown ass $3,500 a month. If I double that, that's $7,000. That's all I'm willing to offer."

"Offer that and see what she says. If she acts like it's not good enough, you better holla at your agent about getting you some more endorsement deals or something. You have two mouths to feed now."

"Yeah. Def come get me tonight because I need a night out. I'm dead ass ready for this season to end, so I can get shit faced every night," I grumbled.

"I feel you man. You have gone through some shit in the past month. Has Afrika or Tyrese tried to reach back out to you?"

"Hell nah, and they need to keep it that way. There's nothing either one of them can ever say to me. I'm slowly getting past it. As soon as the season ends, I'm going to be on somebody's island tuning the world out."

"That sounds like a great idea. Be sure to get some rest and put something heavy on your stomach, 'cus we going the fuck in tonight."

"I'm with it."

Hours later, I was on the passenger side of Bakari's Lamborghini, and I was feeling good as hell. I took three shots before I left the house and speeding down the highway in his car with all my ice on made me realize that I have a life that many people would kill for. I wasn't going to let some unfortunate or unexpected events get me down. I was that nigga, and it was time to start acting like it. Bakari reached in his ashtray and pulled out a joint. He lit it and took a pull. "Season is almost over. We're not gonna get pissed at this point." He took two more pulls and passed it to me.

With the way my life had been going lately, I almost didn't want to take the risk but fuck it. I took a pull from the joint and held the potent weed smoke in my lungs. I exhaled and the THC traveled through my body giving me an almost instant feeling of euphoria. Bakari and I passed the joint back and forth and by the time we arrived at the party, I was faded and smiling at nothing. As soon as he pulled in front of the house, valet approached the car and we got out. The music could be heard from the outside, and I was glad there were no neighbors close by. All kinds of exotic cars lined the street and the driveway, and I could tell this was going to be a dope ass party. Inside, I immediately recognized a few players from the Carolina Panthers and some rappers. A few of my teammates were also there. I spoke to everyone, and a waitress handed me a glass of champagne. Yeah, this shit was going to be fun.

Half-naked women were everywhere vying for the attention of the men present. Women of all different hues, and sizes were at the party, and I instantly began scanning them to see who I wanted for myself. An ebony colored female that stood about 5'7 with a short pixie cut is the one that stood out to me the most. The orange one piece short set that she had on looked perfect against her skin tone. We locked eyes, and she gave me a sultry smile. From there, I knew she was with it. I drained the champagne from my glass and headed for the bar to get a double shot of Crown Royal. As the bartender was handing me the drink, I smelled a floral scented perfume and when I turned my head in the direction of the aroma, I locked eyes once again with orange short set. "What you drinking?" I asked her with hooded lids. It was an open bar, but I'd be a gentleman and order the drink for her.

"I'm a Patron kind of girl."

"Let me get a double shot of Patron," I said to the bartender while placing a twenty dollar bill in the tip jar. She passed me the drink, and I passed it to ole girl.

"Number twenty-five. You're one of my favorite players," she grinned, and I was pleased that she wasn't trying to front like she didn't know who I was.

"I appreciate that. What's your name?"

"Holly. And I was doing some exploring earlier," she stated with a devilish grin. "There's a very nice pool house out back."

Thank God, I had come prepared. There were two condoms in my pocket, and I was with whatever she was with. I downed my drink and let her lead the way out to the pool house. Matt's party was lit for sure because we passed people doing coke, smoking weed, dancing and gyrating all over one another, and quite a few other things. There was no doubt in my mind that fucking was going on in the house, and I was about to join them. The pool house was nice as hell just like Holly said, and it was big enough for a good ten people to fit comfortably inside. There was even a restroom inside it, and we got right down to business as soon as the door was closed behind us. Holly stared me in the eyes as she downed her Patron, then she maintained eye contact as she fumbled with my belt buckle. After unbuttoning my jeans, she reached her soft hand inside my boxer briefs and pulled my semi-hard dick free.

"Ummmm," she smiled down at it, and I was glad that she appeared satisfied.

Holly lowered her body into a squatting position and took me into her mouth. My already low eyelids got lower, but I kept my eyes open. I wanted to watch her give me fellatio. Holly gagged, and I bit my bottom lip. She pulled her head back, released me from her mouth, then spit on my dick. Taking me back into her mouth, she moaned as she sucked my dick, and that shit had my toes curling. She was most certainly a dick sucking professional. The head was sloppy and wet just like I liked it. Holly looked up at me and smiled as spit dripped off her chin. She cleaned my dick off, wiped her mouth, and stood up. That was my cue to put the condom on, and she began to undress.

If the pussy even started feeling too good, I was

going to check and make sure that the condom was still intact. I refused to have another incident where I had to rely on a plan B pill to do a half-assed job. Holly placed her hands flat on the wall, and I walked up behind her and eased up in her. I could tell she was a pro at this one night stand, fuck at first sight shit from her actions, but her pussy told her tale too. It wasn't so loose that I couldn't feel anything, but it was nowhere near tight. This woman must have sex every day of her life several times a day. Her shit dead ass had no grip to it. I like for a woman's vagina to choke my pipe. That was the first disappointment. The second was that her pussy wasn't as wet as I wanted it to be. Shorty had that fye ass head and this mediocre box. I pulled my dick out of her and dropped a glob of spit on my joint. That only made it slightly better. She should have just kept sucking me off. I would rather be sexing Suzon. She was already pregnant by me, so what was the worst that could happen. Plus, since she was already pregnant, I wouldn't have to use condoms. I thought back to the last time we had sex and memories of her sex faces, her moans, and how good she felt is what got me off with Holly.

    I erupted into the condom and pulled out of her immediately. Holly pulled her clothes up and had the nerve to grin at me like she'd just had the time of her life. "Maybe if we exchange numbers, we can do this again sometime."

    I peeled the condom from my dick and stepped into the bathroom. "Nah, I'm straight," I replied before flushing the toilet and washing my hands. When I came out of the bathroom, Holly had a dumbfounded expression on her face.

    "You said what?"

    "I said nah, I'm straight." I fixed my clothes. "That

shit wasn't even all that. You got some good head, but that pussy is garbage," I told her honestly, and she jerked her head back.

"Nigga, fuck you. I for sure hope you don't think your dick is all that," she spat.

I shrugged my shoulders causally. "I can tell from the size of your pussy you're used to much bigger dicks. Don't they sell some kind of cream where you can tighten that shit?" I asked as I breezed past her.

She definitely wasn't worth my time. Oh well, they all can't have good pussy I guess.

Natisha Raynor

Suzon ♥

"I brought you balloons and a card," Mona stepped through my door in a chipper ass mood while I had a scowl on my face. It was my birthday, and it was the worst birthday that I ever had. I didn't have plans because of course, I felt like shit. I got the paternity test results back. I already knew that Esai was the father. If he had gotten the results, he hadn't said anything to me about it, and I wasn't hitting him up. I was mad at the world. My birthday sucked ass.

"Thank you." I didn't mean to sound so dry, but I couldn't fake it. Since Mona knew how I felt, she stopped talking about how I was pregnant with two meal tickets. I had whole ass humans growing in my belly, and they were more than meal tickets. I didn't like that shit, and I made her aware of it.

"Cheer up, baby. I know it's easy for me to say, but this time will fly by. Don't rush it. Are you ready for late night feedings, poopy diapers, and screaming babies?"

I rolled my eyes and flopped down on the couch causing her to laugh. Mona wasn't used to seeing me in such a crabby mood. I hadn't been this sad/irritated since Big Draco died. Papi had sent me $3,000 earlier for my birthday, but I hadn't spoken to him aside from texting him thank you. Not even Mona knew that I fucked with him, and I planned on keeping it to myself.

"Here." She handed me the card, and I opened it. A smile finally graced my face when I saw the $400 inside. "As soon as you feel better, I want you to go pamper yourself. Get a facial, a pedicure, a wax, get your nails done."

I looked down at my nails, and they looked horrible. It took too much energy to sit in a nail shop, so I was going to soak these off and put on some press ons only for when I had to take pictures for promo. Promo was the only reason I even got dressed these days and attempted to look like anything, and I only did that three times a week. "Thank you, Mona. I don't mean to be a bitch, but I've never not celebrated my birthday since I turned eighteen. I always get cute, go out to eat, to the club, and just make my day a big event. My first birthday with Big Draco, he got me four Chanel bags, some Chanel slides, and two tennis bracelets." I had to blink back tears from thinking about him. Another thing that I hated about pregnancy was how emotional it made me. I cried at least once a day.

My phone rang, and I saw that Esai was calling. "Hold on this is Esai. He must have just looked at the paternity results. "Hello?"

"Hey. So, I got the test results. I didn't see them when they first emailed me because I was in practice."

"Yeah. I got them too." I couldn't tell from his voice how he felt. He didn't sound elated, but he didn't sound angry.

"I see on Instagram that it's your birthday. What are you doing?"

"Nothing. Sitting on the couch looking crazy. My night will probably consist of sleeping."

"If it's cool, can I stop by in about an hour?"

I wasn't expecting that. "Sure."

"Aight. I'll see you then."

I raised one eyebrow as I ended the call, and Mona looked at me with wide eyes. "Well, what did he say?" she pried anxiously.

"He said he got the results, asked what I was doing for my birthday, and then he asked if he could stop by in about an hour."

Mona clapped her hands and squealed. "Baby daddy is coming around. Yayyyy. I'm going to get out of here, so you can get cute. Bye boo. Get some birthday dick," she winked her eye, and all I could do was chuckle. Mona was something else.

After she left, I looked down at my black night shirt. I wasn't so sure about getting cute, but I could at least hop in the shower and get fresh. I took a shower and dressed in a black sundress that I had reserved for wearing around the house. In an effort to not look so homely, I even put an ankle bracelet around each ankle and fastened a necklace around my neck. After laying my edges, I added gold hoops to my ears and put clear gloss on my lips. That was as good as it was going to get. The task of getting dressed tired me out, so I sat down on the couch and flipped through channels. My grandparents had called me earlier and wished me happy birthday, but I hadn't heard a peep out of my mother. It was cool though. I grabbed my phone and blocked her number. I would be damned if I allowed her to only call me when she wanted something, and she couldn't even wish her only child a happy birthday.

The doorbell rang, and I let Esai in. He looked handsome as always, and I had to smile at the fact that he was carrying a vase filled with red roses. He also had a large take-out bag in his hands from a Brazilian steakhouse. I couldn't believe that he brought me anything. "Wow, thank you," I stated as I took the vase from him. "These are beautiful. So far, Mona is the only person that even got me anything for my birthday."

Esai's brows furrowed. "You don't have family that you're close with?"

"Nope. My mom only calls me when she wants money, and the day my father left her, he left me too. I have no siblings that I know of, and my grandparents love me, but they're on a fixed income."

"Damn. I'm sorry to hear that."

I shrugged as if it was no big deal, but my feelings were hurt lowkey. I always wondered what I did to deserve a mother like the one that I had. "It is what it is. It's been this way forever. My mom used to buy me birthday gifts when I was little, but since I've been grown, she doesn't get me shit. She's always been a bitch to me, and the day I turned eighteen, it's like she was done. She never even calls just to say hello or ask me how I'm doing. After I started dating Big Draco, she knew how to call and ask me for money though. I just sent her $500 because her neighbor's apartment caught on fire, and she said all of her stuff got smoke damage."

Esai was looking at me like he couldn't believe what I was saying. I simply shook my head. "I know right. Trust me, rich people aren't the only ones that deal with leeches. I know Big Draco cheated on me but aside from my grandparents, he was the only person that ever really made me feel loved or special. He was my first real boyfriend outside of high school. Men would always try to fuck me, but none really wanted to be in a relationship," I confessed sadly. "My mom used to always point out my flaws, so my self-esteem was already low. Every time a man had sex with me then kept it pushing it really made me feel like something was wrong with me. Then, along came Big Draco, and he acted like he couldn't get enough of me." A goofy grin crossed my face, then I realized how dumb I must look, and I stopped grinning. "I'm sorry I'm rambling and dumping all this on you. You must think I'm crazy."

"Not at all. Thank you for sharing. I guess we should know something about each other. We're about to be the parents of two babies. That shit is crazy."

I exhaled deeply. "Tell me about it. One reason that I was so apprehensive about even having one baby is because I don't have a lot of help. We already discussed my mother, and I wouldn't let her baby-sit my kids if she was the last person on Earth. My grandparents might be able to help some but not a lot, and the friends I have," I shook my head. "Let's just say, I think you know they aren't the baby-sitting type. I just felt overwhelmed and like I couldn't do it." I wasn't so sure why I was pouring my heart out to Esai all of a sudden, but he looked really interested in what I was saying.

"You have me, Suzon. I know we don't know each other well, but my parents and I are close, and so is me and my sister. My family will always help out. You won't have to worry about that."

"Thank you." I gave him a genuine smile, and I appreciated him making me feel better. It was good to know that he was willing to help me.

"And I was thinking. Um... would you think $7,000 a month is enough for the babies?" Esai looked like he was holding his breath as he waited on me to answer, and I almost laughed at how nervous he looked.

"$7,000 a month is fine, Esai. I'm just happy you said you and your family would help me. I don't want to have to do this alone. That means a lot to me." I could literally see him breathe a sigh of relief.

"Cool. I can start paying you this month. Every mon—"

I cut him off with a smile. "Esai, you don't have to start helping with the babies financially until they're born. This really isn't all about money with me. I promise."

"I really appreciate you making this easy on me. Some women would have accepted the $7,000 just to start getting something and still would have taken me to court. There are some scandalous ass chicks out here."

"Trust me I know, but everyone isn't the same. I've done some things for money. I'll never front like I'm an angel, but having kids is different. I want this co-parenting thing to go as smoothly as possible. I never imagined that I'd be pregnant by someone that I had sex with on the first night I met them. Talk about embarrassing."

Esai shrugged. "Shit happens. I felt bad when you said you weren't doing anything on your birthday, so I brought food. I don't know what you like, so I got steak, grilled chicken, shrimp, garlic mashed potatoes, asparagus, and house salad."

"Uggggh," I groaned, and his face fell.

"You don't like any of those things?"

"It's not that. I literally eat once a day because I get tired of throwing up. Most of the time, I just drink smoothies and juice. These babies hate everything."

"Damn. I couldn't imagine not being able to eat. Well, at least try to eat a little bit. Hopefully, you can keep something down."

"We shall see," I said as I led him to the kitchen. I grabbed us some plates and rinsed off two forks. I had prepared to spend my birthday in bed asleep and alone, but Esai had offered a nice surprise. I really appreciated him putting forth an effort and not having an attitude about these kids being his. Hopefully, this would be a smooth transition for the both of us.

He opened the containers of food, and I peered at everything. It all looked good but unfortunately, my body didn't belong to me anymore. Fear of throwing up, had me scared to pig out on all of the food that looked absolutely delicious. I grabbed three shrimp, some chicken, and one scoop of potatoes and put it on my plate. I saw Esai looking at me out of the corner of my eye. "What?" I turned towards him and was once again captivated by his handsome features. He was one fine ass man.

"That's all you're going to eat?"

"Listen, you aren't here when I'm puking my guts out, so you might think I'm overreacting. Stick around and if I don't throw this up, I will gladly eat more."

He piled food onto his plate while I poured us some cran-lemonade. We headed back in the living room, and I curled one leg underneath my bottom and sat down. I tasted a small forkful of the potatoes, and they tasted so damn good I almost moaned. I refused to get carried away, so I put one shrimp into my mouth and chewed it slowly while Esai devoured his food.

"Have you thought about what you want? Girls or boys? One of each?" He stopped shoveling food into his mouth long enough to look over at me.

"I've been going through so many different emotions, I haven't really had time to dwell on it, but I really think I want one of each. Once I have these babies, I am never getting pregnant again, and I put that on foe nem."

Esai placed his fist over his mouth and erupted

into laughter. "Yo cut that shit out. You are not gangsta."

I shrugged. "I don't have to be gangsta. That's what they put shit on when they mean it, and I mean this."

Esai continued laughing. "I feel you though. I salute any woman that carries a child period but two at the same time, y'all the real MVP."

"I just keep trying to tell myself that it will all be worth it in the end. I'll have two little innocent faces looking up at me and relying on me for everything. Even though my mother wasn't affectionate or loving, my grandmother was, and she showed me what a good mother should be. I will never let my kids feel how my mother has made me feel time and time again. My kids will know unconditional love and respect," I vowed.

"I can dig it. I haven't thought about when I'm going to tell my family, but my mom is going to be geeked for sure. Twins? She already has my niece and my nephew spoiled rotten. They're six and seven. She bakes for them almost every day, and she goes to get them almost every weekend."

I smiled. I was so happy that he came from a good family. I wasn't worried about them liking me or any of that. As long as they treated my kids well, I didn't give a damn how they felt about me. "I just know that if these kids mess my body up and I can't go back to making money how I am now, I'm suing you," I joked.

Esai chuckled. "You better start doing promo for BBW clothes."

That made me laugh, and I couldn't believe that I was having fun with him. We were vibing, and it wasn't forced at all. "Tell me more about your family."

I ate my food slow while Esai talked to me about his parents and his sister. He even told me about how his ex cheated on him in his house and how his sister went and whooped her ass. My mouth fell open in shock. "In your house? Ahh man. That was foul as hell. Imagine how many times they've done that in your bed."

Esai's jaw muscles clenched together, and I could tell just the thought had him furious. I didn't think anybody deserved that shit. Damn. "It's been a month, and I still want to choke both of them with my bare hands."

"Well, I commend you for not doing it. Don't let anybody mess up everything that you've worked hard for. People will deserve everything they have coming to them and still run to the police after they get it because they want a reason to sue."

"That's the fucked up thing about it. At a time in my life where I have to question damn near everybody and figure out if they have a motive, I just knew I had those two people in my life that I knew before the money and the fame, and I just knew that I could trust them with my life. They fooled the hell out of me." Esai shook his head, and I could tell he was truly bothered.

"My own mother taught me that no one is above doing you dirty. I know that had to hurt. She could have at least gone to his house or gone to a hotel room, but we don't have to keep talking about that. I'm just glad I haven't thrown up yet. I pray this stays down, and thank you for making my birthday special. I cried earlier because it's the lamest birthday I ever had. These babies make me cry about everything."

"It's no problem. I feel like we should at least be friends."

"I'm with that."

"This might sound kind of fucked up but..." Esai's voice trailed off, and he looked uncomfortable.

I was curious about what he had to say. My eyebrows hiked up, and I glared at him. "What?"

"Never mind. You always talk about being sick, I don't want to come off as insensitive."

"You want some pussy?"

Esai laughed. "Why you had to say it like that? I'm just saying it crossed my mind a time or two. Especially since you're already pregnant, and I don't have to use condoms."

I placed my plate on the coffee table and stood up. "You better be glad I was able to keep that food down." I eyed him, and he looked confused for a moment but finally, he got it. Esai stood up and followed me to my bedroom.

The times we had sex before, he wasn't big on foreplay, so I was shocked when he invaded my personal space and put his lips on mine. His tongue probed my mouth, and he rubbed my ass through my dress. My nipples got hard, and it was the first time I was sexually aroused since being pregnant. I wasn't even into it the night I did it with Papi. I just did it. This time though, my body grew warm, and my clit swelled from the kiss that I was sharing with Esai. He slid the spaghetti straps of my dress off my shoulders, and I let my dress fall to the floor.

"My breasts are sore as hell," I stated in a voice just above a whisper, and he placed gentle kisses on my swollen breasts.

I loved the feel of his lips on my skin, and I was more than ready to feel Esai inside of me. He must have felt the same way about me because he stepped back and began to undress. I lay back on the bed and in no time, he was climbing in between my legs. Our lips met again, and we kissed as he entered me. My vagina was super sensitive, and his entry damn near hurt me. It felt as if my pussy had gotten tighter, and his girth was new to me. I moaned into his mouth as he eased into me inch by inch.

"Fuuccckkk," Esai whispered, and I knew that I felt good to him.

I peered up into his face and watched him with his hooded lids and his mouth that was slightly agape. "Ummmm," I moaned as he pushed in and pulled out of me with slow and steady strokes. I was wet as hell and getting wetter by the second.

Esai looked down at me as if he was amazed. "Fuck Suzon."

My name sounded so good coming off his lips. He slammed into me a bit harder and slightly faster, and I cried out from an orgasm that felt like it started in my toes. "Shiittttt," he groaned as he came with me and all in me.

His body jerked slightly, and he looked down at me as if he was just seeing me for the first time. "Shit. I can't even be embarrassed. I haven't had any raw pussy in a minute, and your shit is too good. Plus, I'm sober. I haven't cum that fast in a long time."

I giggled. "It's okay. I've always heard that pregnant coochie is good."

"Man. Whoever said that ain't never lied."

Esai slid out of me, and his dick looked like a glazed doughnut. He headed into my bathroom and cleaned himself off. I stood up, so I could get in the shower. I went over to my dresser and pulled out panties and something to sleep in. Esai came out of the bathroom and started to get dressed. "I'll leave the rest of that food here for you."

"Thank you. I'm gonna get in the shower. I'll lock

the door once I get out. This is a pretty secure building, so it should be fine."

"Okay. Happy birthday."

I smiled at him. "Thank you."

In the shower, I smiled. This was the most that I smiled since finding out I was pregnant. I truly enjoyed Esai. I was glad that we were getting along. I didn't want to jump the gun because he made it clear after his girl cheated that he was good on relationships, and maybe I was too. I missed Big Draco but at the end of the day, being in a relationship with a high profile man is draining. Maybe I should just be happy with the friendship and focus on getting into nail school and my kids. I could worry about love later in life. My pussy throbbed making me remember how Esai felt in between my thighs. My baby daddy had some good ass dick. Once my body was clean, I got out of the shower and wrapped a fluffy black towel around myself. I moisturized my face then put lotion on my body. I pulled a white nightshirt over my head and put on some peach colored panties. I went to lock the door and was startled to see Esai in the living room sitting on the couch.

"Boy, you scared me. I thought you were gone."

He stood up. "Nah. I want one more round." He walked over to me and kissed me all the way back to my bedroom.

ESAI 🏀

I was going to ease out quietly the next morning, so I wouldn't disturb Suzon, but she was up at six am throwing up. She sounded like she was going through in the bathroom. I sat up and listened to her, and it sounded disgusting. I needed to get home and eat breakfast and make a smoothie before heading to practice. There's no way I can get through five hours of intense practice without eating a nutritious breakfast. I don't eat healthy all the time, but there's no way I can be at the top of my game by not being in shape and in good health, so I really try to watch what I put in my body. I heard the toilet flush, and I stood in the bathroom doorway and found Suzon brushing her teeth. Her eyes were red like she'd been crying.

"You good?"

"Yeah. This is just how they say good morning," she joked dryly.

"I have practice in two and a half hours, so I'm about to run home."

"Okay. I'll probably make a smoothie and get back in bed."

I damn near felt sorry for Suzon. She went from being a carefree party girl to staying in the house all the time because she was sick and felt bad. She had a long way to go too. I left her condo and headed home. I didn't want to get a speeding ticket, but I took my chances and broke the speed limit all the way there. Being late for practice would have coach on my ass, and I didn't need that. Suzon lived about twenty minutes from me, and I lived fifteen minutes from practice. Even with morning traffic, I made it home in fourteen minutes. I had taken a shower at her place the night before, so I raced up the stairs and threw on some basketball shorts and a tank top. I scrambled two eggs with spinach and made some whole wheat toast. I topped it off with a grapefruit and once I scarfed that down, I made a smoothie and put two bottles of water on the counter. I then went upstairs to brush my teeth, wash my face, and grab my bag. The entire way to practice, I thought about my evening with Suzon. She was cool as hell and once I got to know some things about her, I felt bad for thinking that she wanted to have a baby by me to come up. I could believe the things she said about her mom because I have teammates that have parents that are the same way. Don't really give a damn about them but always have their hand out for money.

 I thank God that my parents aren't like that. No one in my family is. Even though me and Suzon were in a better place, I was still going to wait a few months before I told my family about the babies. She seemed to understand where I was coming from about not wanting to be in a relationship, and her pussy already had me addicted. I didn't have to wear a condom?! Hands down, that was enough of a reason for me to prefer her over other women. I was still going to have my fun though. I was serious when I said I would be fifty before I settled back down. I prayed that me and Suzon could keep our cool lil' co-parenting thing going without the drama and the bull, but only time would tell.

 I arrived at practice ten minutes early, so I cash

apped her $7,000. I sat in my car looking at my phone screen. I had really sent this girl $7,000. I got out of my car with my bag and hit the lock button on my key fob when Suzon called my phone. "Yo."

"I told you that you don't have to give me money until these babies are born, and I meant that."

I felt corny as fuck when I smiled at her deep, sleep filled voice. She even sounded sexy when she was half-asleep. "I know what you told me, and it wasn't for the babies. It was for your birthday. Get some rest. I'll check on you later."

"Okay. Bye."

"Maybe this baby mama thing wouldn't be so bad after all."

I had three away games back to back, so I didn't see Suzon for two weeks after her birthday, but we talked on the phone every day. The third game was out in LA, and I was glad to be heading back home with a break from games for a few days. The season was almost over, and I felt I had done a damn good job of proving that I was worth a fat ass contract despite all I'd been through. I put that shit behind me and gave it my best on the court, and I was proud of myself. Me and my teammates hit a bar, and after my third shot, ZaZa slid into my DM's. I flirted with her for a minute then told her to come to the hotel bar. I would for sure fuck her sexy ass, leave town, and not speak to her again unless I was in LA or she was in NC.

"How is that situation going?" Bakari leaned in and asked me while Dip, Rod, and a few of our other teammates were engaged in conversation and not thinking about what we were saying.

I took a sip of my tequila. "It's been pretty cool

actually. We've been vibing really well, and I offered her the $7,000. She said it was enough and when I offered to start paying her this month, she said I don't have to start giving her money for the babies until they're born."

Bakari's eyebrows hiked up. "That's what's up. She's only what, two months? She could have been getting an easy seven g's a month just for being pregnant, and she told you that was aight? You just might have a keeper."

"I hope so. I really hope she doesn't front like she's cool then flip the script on me. She even told me how she's scared she won't have help because her and her mom aren't close, and her grandparents are up there in age. When I told her my family would help, she looked mad relieved. I'll admit that I don't know her that well, but it seems like she'll be a good mom."

"At the end of the day, that's all you can ask for. Some of these groupies are hell on two feet. You could have gotten hit with a hoe that's asking for money for a maid, a chef, a nanny, designer maternity clothes, and all that shit. My baby mama bought a $3,900 highchair. When I tell you I can't stand that broad."

I chuckled because Bakari hates his ex almost as much as I hate Afrika. Our conversation continued for a bit, and then I noticed him looking past me with a lustful gleam in his eyes. I looked over my shoulder and saw ZaZa. All eyes were on her, and I stood up to greet her, grateful that she wasn't a catfish. She didn't have on tons of make-up, and she looked just as good as she did on IG. As soon as she sat down, I waved the bartender over, and ZaZa ordered a drink. I planned to get shit faced and see what that pussy was like. Not only did I have a box of condoms, but I also had a plan B pill. If we had a slip up, there would be no waiting until the next day. I would watch her swallow that muhfucka, then I would make sure she didn't throw up.

"What time does your flight leave?" she asked as she sized me up with a sly smirk on her face. I absolutely love meeting women that's with the shits right out the gate. We don't have to fake wine and dine and shit. From the moment the conversation starts, both parties already know what's going down. And the trippy part is, a lot of the women don't even want money. They simply just want to sex a famous nigga.

"Seven am." My eyelids felt heavy, and I knew I was lit. One more drink would get me where I needed to be.

ZaZa glanced at her Cartier watch. "That means we have around seven hours to do what we do."

"It's gon' take that long, huh?"

ZaZa poked the inside of her cheek with her tongue. "I hope so."

She smelled good as hell like vanilla and cinnamon. ZaZa threw her shot back and didn't even flinch. It might not have been something I should pray to God about, but I really hoped her pussy was better than Holly's. If it was better than Suzon's I just might marry her. Or at the very least fly her out to NC for some house calls. I ordered us more drinks, and we sucked them down before heading towards the elevator. All eyes were on ZaZa's ass, and my teammates were patting me on the back like I was off to do some great deed. I don't think she minded. In fact, she liked the attention. If the sex was good, I would even give some referrals and let the other members of the team hit her up. In the elevator, she backed her ass up on me. Shorty wasn't shy at all. I placed my hands on her thighs as she gyrated on me. In the room, I damn near stumbled trying to kick my sneakers off. I wanted out of my clothes as soon as possible. As soon as my ass hit the bed, ZaZa's mouth was on my dick. I wasn't erect yet, but after less than a minute of her deep throating me, I was at my full-length. "Ouuu he gets big," she smiled wide with my dick still in her mouth.

"Do that shit," I coached her with a low growl as she laced my tool with salvia.

ZaZa gave my balls some attention as she circled them with her tongue then popped them in and out of her mouth. "You taste so good," she moaned, and I appreciated the fact that she acted like my penis was the best thing that she ever tasted. She was devouring my dick and complimenting it at the same time, and that shit had my toes curling.

As amazing as her head was, after three minutes I was ready to fuck. "Let me see what your ride game is like," I stated as I reached over for a condom.

"I ride better than an equestrian, and I have my latest STD results in my bag. I got checked for everything two weeks ago. We don't need that," her eyes fell on the gold wrapper that was nestled between my fingers.

Being that I was heavily under the influence, I almost called her ass out of her name. I may have been drunk, but I still knew what I was doing. "Nah, love. We gon' use this rubber or we can't fuck," I stated adamantly. Her head wasn't that good to make me lose all common sense.

ZaZa pouted. I mean, her lips were sticking out further than a kid that got her candy taken away. She was about to make my dick deflate with her childish scheming ass. Just when I was about to toss her ass out of my room, she straddled me, and I placed the protection on my pipe. Zaza was wet and much tighter than Holly, and her snug box made my attitude go away instantly. She traced my neck with her tongue as she rode the hell out of me. The sound of me smacking her ass cheeks hard as hell could be heard echoing throughout my hotel suite. Each time my hand connected with her flesh, her moans got louder, and I knew she liked that rough shit. I sat up and tossed her over roughly. I could tell her blonde curly hair was hers, so after I slid into her from behind, I grabbed a handful of her shit and started pounding her aggressively. ZaZa let out deep, throaty moans that were coming out choppy. She had an orgasm that had her screaming so loud, I damn near put my hand over her mouth.

Her cries drowned out the sound of our bodies smacking together. My balls slapped her pussy with each stroke, and my stroke game was so ill, she was calling on the Lord repeatedly. We switched positions several more times and finished the sexcapade off with her on her knees and me cumming down her throat. I preferred it that way because I didn't have to worry about accidents. My orgasm left me breathing hard and sweaty. I wanted to take a shower, and I wasn't leaving her unattended in my room while I was in the bathroom.

"I need to shower and hit the sack, so I can be up early to catch my flight. I had fun though. I'll have to fly you out when I want to do it again."

I saw the disappointment flicker in her eyes. She wasn't spending the night, and I didn't want to go anymore rounds. I had just played in a whole damn basketball game. Between that, all the shots I had and sex, I was exhausted. ZaZa accepted defeat easily, and she got dressed without a word. I let her out and hit the shower. I had just gotten settled in bed and closed my eyes when my phone started going off. I was going to ignore the notifications, but something told me to check them. As soon as I opened IG, I wished that I hadn't. I stared at my phone screen wondering just how much these people were going to put me through. When was the shit going to stop? In the picture wearing a hoodie with her head down was Afrika getting into Tyrese's car. The car I bought her was still in my driveway, and I planned on selling it. It wasn't even just her being with Tyrese that bothered me. Him and Afrika were spotted leaving the OBGYN. Was this hoe pregnant?

Suzon ♥

    I stared at the picture of Esai and some blonde bitch getting on a hotel elevator, and I wasn't sure why I was bothered. He wasn't my man. Shit, I barely knew him. He also made it perfectly clear that he didn't want to be in a relationship. He was a handsome athlete, and he was rich. I'm sure he bedded a different woman every night of the week, and that was none of my concern. All I cared about was him being on board with me having these kids because him being an ass about it wouldn't make my life any easier. I got up off the couch and went to the kitchen to get a banana. I refused to sit in the house all day laid up in bed sleeping and feeling miserable. If I had to live the next seven months like this, I'd pull all of my hair out. I was going to do just what Mona suggested and at least pamper myself. I also knew that in no time at all, I'd be wide as all outside, so I might even go shopping for some cute little dresses. I didn't give a damn what I did. I had to get out of the house. I managed to keep the banana down, so I drank some orange juice and took my iron pill and vitamins.
    After making my bed, I dressed in some red spandex shorts and a red off the shoulder shirt. I put my faux locs up in a bun and wrapped a scarf around my head. I wasn't going to use all of the money that Esai had given me but since he said it was for my birthday and not the babies, who wasn't about to treat herself to something? He made my birthday a good one, but it was

still nowhere near as lit as my other birthdays had been. My first stop was the nail salon where I got a fill-in, pedicure, and I got my eyebrows waxed. The next stop was to get a Brazilian wax, and I also got my arm pits waxed. It hurt like a bitch, but I'm not with all that shaving every few days. By the time I left the spa, I was feeling a little nauseous and tired, but the fresh air was doing me some good. And I felt like I was getting back to me a bit. I stopped by Chic-fil-a and got some chicken noodle soup and crackers. I was so happy that I hadn't thrown up yet, that alone had me in a good mood.

    I went to the mall and bought three dresses, three pairs of leggings and three tops, three pairs of sandals, and some perfume. It had been a good day indeed, and I was ready to go home. At home, I showered, put on some black and white Nike leggings and a matching sports bra, lit some candles and made a smoothie. I went out on my balcony and took a few selfies. Back inside my condo, I had just gotten comfortable on the couch when the doorbell rang.

    "Are you kidding me?" I groaned. It had been a pretty good day, but it had tired my ass out. I knew I would more than likely be on the couch for the rest of the day. Wondering who the hell was at my door, I walked over with smoothie in hand, and looked through the peephole. Shock set in as my eyes landed on Esai. I hadn't expected to see him, and I was surprised that he didn't ask if he could come by first.

    I slowly opened the door, and I noticed right away that he was drunk. His red rimmed eyes and the smell of vodka coming through his pores told on him before he even opened his mouth. I scrunched up my nose at the stench of Grey Goose. My sense of smell was heightened since being pregnant, and most smells made me sick on the stomach. I took a step back to let him in. "Did you bathe in Grey Goose?"

He looked up at me in shock. "You can tell what kind of liquor I was drinking?"

The scowl remained on my face. "Yes. It's coming all through your pores. You drove like that?"

Esai stepped inside my condo, and I closed the door behind him. "Man, my life is all fucked up." Esai stumbled right over to my couch and flopped down on it. "My ex is pregnant. She was at the doctor with Tyrese. That better not be my fuckin' baby. What am I gonna do with three kids? But better yet if it's his, how she gon' be pregnant by my man? Huh?" He peered at me like he really wanted me to answer that question.

I could tell he was hurt. I would never deal with Papi if Big Draco was alive, but I was essentially doing the same thing. I was sleeping with his best friend, and that shit was foul. I wasn't proud of it at all, and I prayed that no one ever found out. I sat down beside Esai praying to God that he didn't start crying. That would be awkward as hell. "Have you tried to talk to her? Simply ask her whose child it is. Like I told you, I'm not trying to take all your money or make you support me along with these kids. I can't speak for what she'd do, but as long as you help me, I'd never put you on child support. Juggling three small kids would be hard, but you can do it." I was trying to think of anything to make him feel better.

"Talk to her? I don't want to hear her voice or see her face. I'm tired of seeing that bitch in the blogs. Every time I'm not thinking about her, I have to get tagged in some shit on Instagram. I hate that bitch!"

I wasn't sure what to say, but I didn't have to say anything. Esai hopped up off the couch, flew in the bathroom, and threw up. I shook my head. He had overdone it for real. His phone was going off crazy, and I glanced down at the screen since his phone was right on the couch. He had so many DM's on IG and Snapchat the shit was crazy, and they were all from females. I for damn sure didn't miss dealing with that shit. Mad women want a famous nigga, but the average woman could never handle the stress of it. Not at all. His ass didn't even have to be cute. As long as he had status and money, women would damn near rape them in an effort to say they've been with them. It's insane. I can be categorized as groupie myself simply from hanging with Mona and putting myself in the position to have sex with Esai, but I didn't meet Big Draco on no groupie shit. He got at me. After him, Papi was a mistake that lasted way too long, and Esai was the only other famous guy I had. I don't plan on my life being over after I have these kids, but my days of running with Mona and trying to find a baller to fuck with will be over for the most part. Unless I'm getting paid, I can't be that mother that's in the clubs and in the streets more than they're at home with their kids.

    I realized that Esai hadn't come out of the bathroom yet, so I got up and went looking for him. I found him stretched out on my bed which is where he needed to be. He for sure needed to sleep that shit off. I took his shoes off and went back in the living room. I put his phone on my coffee table and got comfortable to take a nap my damn self. I dosed off instantly, and when I woke up, I could tell that it was dark outside. I looked at the table, and Esai's phone was still there. I was shocked that he was still asleep, but then I heard him in the bathroom gargling with mouth wash. My bladder was about to burst, so I went in while he was in there and pulled my leggings down.

"Sorry but I gotta go. You've seen my private parts anyway," I joked.

Esai shook his head. "Man, I feel like shit. I can't believe I let myself drink that much. I don't even remember driving here. That shit is insane."

"Not to mention dangerous," I chastised him. "You can't do that again, Esai."

He chuckled and looked over at me. "Yes ma'am. My birthday is September 1st."

I furrowed my eyebrows and rolled some tissue off. "Okay. You want a gift?" I was trying to figure out why he randomly mentioned his birthday.

Esai leaned against the counter. "I just can't get over the fact that I'm having kids with someone that I don't know. I of course, know when your birthday is, but I don't even know your last name. Unless you goggled some shit, you don't know much about me either."

"I know, but we have seven more months to correct that. My last name is Lattimore." I washed my hands, and we walked back in the living room. "Your phone has been blowing up, and I only touched it to move it from the couch."

Esai grabbed his phone, flopped down, and went straight to his DoorDash app. "You hungry? I want some wings or something."

I scrunched up my face as I thought about his question. I would give anything to be able to keep down some wings and some fries, but just the thought of all that grease made me queasy. "I'll just eat some applesauce or something."

Esai shook his head. "You're going to be the size of a twelve year old if you don't start eating. I'll at least order you some fries. You won't know if you can keep it down unless you eat it first."

I didn't respond because pregnancy had me with a short-temper. I could get real snappy, and I didn't want to go there with Esai. He didn't know how it felt to be pregnant, so he couldn't offer any suggestions. I was going to appease him and eat some fries and if I threw them up, I was going to punch him in the face. Simple.

"So, you're not going to contact your ex and ask if that's your baby?"

"Nope. If she wanted me to know, she would tell me." Esai didn't look up from his phone. I knew he was irritated, but he was being immature in my opinion.

"The way you got sloppy drunk, it's clearly bothering you. For peace of mind, I think you should have a two second conversation with her. That's better than drinking your troubles away."

Esai finally looked over at me. "No offense, but it really isn't any of your concern. I said I don't want to talk to the bitch."

That pissed me off, but I remained calm. "Say less." My tone was even and respectful, but he had me fucked up. I got up off the couch and went in my bedroom. He didn't have to be here. I didn't even give him permission to come through. Dumb ass nigga. I turned my TV and looked for something to watch with a scowl on my face. I held my face in that position for so long, I started to get a headache.

I exhaled a deep breath and scrolled through IG. Mona was having the time of her life on yet another vacation. Alara was somewhere in a club smoking hookah. Everyone that I knew was out somewhere living their best life, and I was home in bed about to eat some damn fries. I wouldn't even care that I couldn't smoke or drink if I just had the energy to go out. This pregnancy shit was some bullshit. When I got tired of watching people have fun on social media, I turned my attention towards the movie I had chosen. Esai appeared in my bedroom door.

"I'm sorry. I shouldn't have said that to you. I brought my troubles to you, and you were just trying to help. Forgive me?"

I appreciated the apology, but he still got on my nerves. I simply stuck my tongue out at him, and he laughed. "You childish as hell. Come back in here with me. Please."

I huffed like he was getting on my nerves, but I lowkey wanted to smile. After turning the TV off, I eased off the bed and followed him into the living room. The doorbell rang, and he got the food from the delivery driver. I sat down on the couch, and he pulled the containers of food from the bag. Esai sat right beside me and passed me my fries. He was mad close to me, and it was making me slightly nervous. I played it cool though and popped a fry into my mouth. It was fresh and hot, and I closed my eyes. I hadn't had fries since I found out I was pregnant. "This is so good," I moaned.

When I opened my eyes back up, I saw that Esai was holding a chicken wing in front of my face. "Take a bite."

Him feeding me made my heart flutter. I leaned in and took a bite. "That is so good," I eyed the wing in his hand. He chuckled and gave me the whole thing.

Esai and I ate and watched TV pretty much in silence. Once we were done, he turned to look at me. "You didn't throw up. I think my kids like it when I feed you."

"Yeah, okay," I said skeptically. "Don't speak too soon. If I don't do it tonight, it will for sure wake me up bright and early in the morning."

Esai peered at me as if he was studying me. "You look nice today. I meant to tell you that when I first came in."

I blushed like a schoolgirl with a crush. "Thank you. I pampered myself some today."

He leaned in and placed his face in the crook of my neck, and my breathing became labored. "You smell good too."

"Thank you," I whispered as he began to suck on my neck. My eyes fluttered closed, as I enjoyed the feel of his lips on my skin.

I'm not sure why images of him on the elevator with the blonde chick flashed into my mind. What did it matter? He wasn't mine. But is this what it was going to be? We hang out in private, have sex, and then he does him out in the world while I'm here sick or raising kids? I decided I was reading too much into it. Esai placed a finger under my chin and turned my face towards his. We engaged in a passionate kiss that had me leaking in a matter of seconds. We ended up in my bed with our fingers intertwined as he eased in and out of me. I was becoming addicted to his smell, his touch, his voice, his kisses, hell, his presence. Mona's voice echoed through my head as if a record was playing.

"These niggas aren't Big Draco. Chances are slim to none that they will wife you, so get your money, and don't be shy about it."

Esai wasn't trying to wife me, but we damn sure ended up being more than a one night stand. After we had sex, Esai rolled off of me and snuggled up behind me on the bed. Talk about mixed messages. I hate when men that say they don't want to be in relationships start doing relationship type shit.

"Did you have fun in LA?" I found myself asking. I wasn't trying to start any shit, but it was on the tip of my tongue. I needed to know if he was going to make it a habit of being with random females one day and in my bed the next.

"You talking about the chick on the elevator? Is that a problem?"

"How can that be a problem? You're single. I just asked if you had fun."

"Something told me that question was sarcastic as hell, but yeah, it was aight. I use protection when I'm with other women, and I made it clear that I didn't want a relationship, right?"

I turned to face him. "Yes, you did, but let's get something straight. I like having sex with you. It's not like I'm going to be having sex with anyone else, but if you don't want to be in a relationship, act like it. I can't do that mixed signals shit. Not while these babies have me emotional as hell. So, we can have sex but no spending the night and cuddling. No popping up without permission. You can't do to me anything that I can't do to you," I put my foot down.

Esai's eyebrows hiked up. "I guess that's fair. I can't even be mad. So, you kicking me out?"

"No, I'm not kicking you out. Just don't fall asleep."

"Damn, it's a cold world, but I can respect it." Esai got out of my bed and began to get dressed.

I stared at him wishing he could stay, but I couldn't let being pregnant with his babies make me loose all my common sense. If he didn't want to be in a relationship, he wasn't going to act like we were in one behind closed doors. That's where I had to put my foot down.

ESAI

As soon as I pulled up in Tyrese's driveway and saw his car, my adrenaline started pumping. I knew I shouldn't be on his property looking for trouble, but I had used every ounce of self-restraint that I had. The more I thought about Afrika possibly being pregnant, the more it made my blood boil. It may have been a stupid move on my part, but I would deal with the consequences later. Whatever they may be. My heart beat rapidly in my chest as I knocked on Tyrese's door. A few seconds later, he answered the door looking surprised to see me.

"Esai, what's up?" Nigga looked scared as hell, but he was trying to play it cool. All the color had drained from his light-skinned ass face.

I yanked the screen door open causing him to step back. Tyrese lives in an upscale neighborhood in a $300,000 house, and I didn't want to risk his neighbors calling the police when they saw me on his ass. "Is Afrika pregnant?" I barked with my fists clenched at my sides.

Tyrese took a step back. "Esai—"

"Answer the question!" I barked cutting him off. I already knew the answer though. The way he didn't answer me right away told me everything that I needed to know, and that shit hurt. It felt like a dagger had been placed in the center of my chest. After damn near ten years in a relationship, we were both about to have kids with other people. Wasn't this some shit? At least I assumed we were both having kids by other people.

"Y-yes. We just found the other day."

Out of the corner of my eye, I saw a figure appear and when I looked up and saw Afrika, I lost it. I literally blacked out for at least a minute and when I zoned back in, Tyrese was on his back on the floor, and I was punching him over and over in the face while Afrika screamed and cried in the background. She was so frantic, that she was jumping up and down. I looked down and saw blood pouring from Tyrese's nose, and I stopped hitting him. I couldn't lose my career over this shit. I couldn't lose anymore of my life than I already had. I backed up as if I was in a trance, and Tyrese scrambled to get up off the floor. He held his shirt up to his bloody nose, and I just stared at him.

"Esai, I'm sorry. If that made you feel better then I'm glad you did it," he had a nerve to mumble, and I had to get out of there.

I got in my car and raced down the residential street like I was on a racetrack. My knuckles were throbbing, but I barely felt the pain. I still didn't understand the purpose of shit happening like this. Maybe it was just the way that things had to be in order for my twins to be born. For whatever reason, Suzon was supposed to be their mother and not Afrika. God has a sense of humor for sure. This was one of those times where being famous was a pain in the ass because I didn't really want to go home and drink alone, but I didn't like being out in bars and shit alone. I couldn't risk getting too drunk and slipping. Niggas would love to go back to the hood bragging about how they robbed me or anybody else with a little fame and bread. I wasn't going to run to Suzon's place either.

I can't even front. I was feeling like since she was already pregnant by me, I could just take advantage of that and lay up and do my thing in private whenever I wanted, but she shut that down quick. I couldn't be mad at her though because I didn't want to do anything that might make her fall in love with my ass. Afrika was the last female that would ever get the chance to say she played me, and I meant that. I was just going to go home and drink my sorrows away like I had been doing. I had one more game in the season and as soon as it was over, I was boarding a plane to go somewhere far away from the bullshit and the madness that had become my life.

I discreetly looked over and saw Suzon and Mona sitting courtside. I had invited her to my last game. All she does now is sit in the house, and I felt bad about that shit. She was holding a bottle of water looking good as hell dressed in a white off the shoulder dress and red strappy heels. She had taken her faux locs out, and she had a black bob with a part down the middle. She had make-up on her face, and a Christian Dior bag sat at her feet. Suzon fit right in with the other wives and girlfriends sitting courtside. I wasn't even going to call her a groupie. Seeing as how she was going to be the mother of my kids, I didn't want to keep referring to her as that. She was proving otherwise to me because she still hadn't asked me for a dime, and I really believed that she wouldn't put me on child support.

After I sobered up the other night and really thought about what I did, I had to admit that I was dumb as fuck for beating Tyrese's ass the way I did. He could have easily gone to the police, and Afrika would have been his witness. It hurts that they still deal with each other but a criminal charge could have resulted in me losing my career as a ball player. At the end of the day, I'd rather lose Afrika ten times over than to lose basketball. I made a vow to myself to never go near either one of them again. They could have each other and live happily ever after for all I cared. I couldn't just get over it like that, but it was time to put Afrika and Tyrese behind me. I blocked everything out and played my best. We won the game and overall, I scored twenty-two points. Just like that, I had completed a season, and I was free to do me. In an effort to remain discreet, Suzon left the game with Mona, and I met them a few miles up the road, and Suzon got in the car with me to go to my house.

"Congratulations on your win," she smiled at me.

"Thank you. I'm celebrating tonight with a big ass blunt."

A lot of my teammates were getting together and getting drunk among other things, but I was content kicking it with Suzon. I got us food and at my house, I took two shots and rolled a blunt while she ate. Her stomach was still pretty much flat, but her face had picked up a little weight. With the weight gain in her ass and breasts, she overall looked a little chunkier, but she was still fine as hell. Kicking my feet up and smoking in peace was the best feeling ever. I zoned out and thought about where I was going on vacation to. I also wrestled with whether or not I should invite Suzon or if I should just fuck some locals whenever I got to where I was going. By the time I finished the blunt, I had decided on Dubai. I looked over at Suzon, and she was asleep. I found myself just staring at her. Shorty was gorgeous as fuck. If I wasn't fresh out of a break-up, and if I didn't feel like women were trifling ass sack chasers, I just might try to make her mine. I couldn't see myself being in another relationship though. Afrika had been playing me for the longest time, and I had no damn clue. I trusted her grimy ass just that much, and it tripped me the fuck out.

Suzon's phone was at her side going off crazy. I wasn't going to go through her shit. I mean, we're not in a relationship, so why did it matter what she did? And it had been proven that the babies were mine. Her shit was more than likely locked anyway. Bit what if Mona was telling her to do some sack chasing shit like go through my things. Maybe they were plotting on how Suzon could get over on me in some way. All kinds of things started running through my mind as I just stared at her phone. The screen lit up every few seconds, and it was really eating me up inside wondering who was texting her back to back like that. I picked my glass up and threw back all of the tequila that was in it. I frowned my face up at the taste as I placed the glass back down and looked right back over at the phone. The liquor didn't help because when playing devil's advocate, the alcohol will always rule in the devil's favor.

Instinctively, I grabbed her phone and saw that most of the texts were from Papi. My brows furrowed in confusion as I wondered if it was Papi the rapper or just some nigga that she called Papi. Suzon is nowhere near being my girl, but just the thought of her calling some nigga that shit made my blood boil. Being that her phone was locked, I only could see a portion of the messages that were coming through, but I didn't have to see the entire message to know that he was blowing her up because he wanted to see her. He was in town, and he was wondering where she was. Then a cash app came through for $1,900, and I damn near lost it.

"Suzon!" I barked her name so aggressively that

she jumped, and her eyes flew open. She looked scared as hell as she peered at me with a confused expression on her face. Her eyes fell on her phone than came back up to my face.

"Why are you yelling? And why do you have my phone?" She sat all the way up.

"Please tell me you aren't out here selling pussy while you're pregnant with my kids," I stated through clenched teeth. Just when I was thinking her ass was cool, she went and messed it all up. Bitches aren't shit.

"What the fuck are you talking about?" she snapped. Now, she was angry, but I didn't give a damn.

I tossed her phone at her. "Papi is in town, and he wants to see you. The nigga also sent you $1,900. I thought you didn't have a price?" I looked at her with all the hatred I felt for Afrika and then some. I couldn't believe I almost let her trife ass fool me.

"First of all, I don't sell pussy! Papi and I messed around for a bit, and he always gives me money. We don't see each other regularly, and he doesn't know I'm pregnant."

"Papi the rapper?" I continued to stare a hole into her.

"Yes." She had the nerve to look ashamed. She couldn't even look me in the eyes when she answered, and she looked the other way as I let out a sarcastic chuckle.

"Big Draco and Papi were close as hell, right? They've done how many songs together? Papi is always shouting that man out. Wow. What is it with you hoes and best friends?"

Suzon's head whipped in my direction. "Watch who the fuck you're calling a hoe. I can admit that it's wrong, but Big Draco isn't alive. I didn't fuck Papi in that man's house, so don't use your situation to judge me. You don't know shit about me. Big Draco cheated on me plenty. I still love him, but life goes on."

"Y'all always use the excuse that a nigga cheated. So just leave! You think cheating back makes you look good?"

"I didn't cheat on him. He's dead asshole!"

"I don't care how you try to spin it. Sleeping with that man's friend is foul. That's why you aren't that pressed to get money until the babies are born. You got other niggas out here sending you bread. How many niggas are you fucking, Suzon?!"

"Boy fuck you! You're going to think what you want to think anyway! Papi was the first and only nigga I slept with after Big Draco passed, and you were the second. That's it! I don't sell pussy!"

"You sold some to me."

"I'm out." She stood up and grabbed her things angrily. "I swear to God I wish I had the kind of heart where I didn't give a fuck about certain shit or these babies would never see the light of day. I hate to keep saying that but having to deal with you for eighteen years isn't something I look forward to. I can't stand your ass. Maybe your personality is why your ex cheated on you. Bastard," she yelled as she headed for the door.

That wounded my ego and hurt my pride something terrible. "You might be right. And it might be why God hates me enough to let me have not one but two babies by a sack chasing, cum guzzling, whore that's running through the industry. Fuckin' slut," I seethed.

Suzon turned around and headed back towards me furiously. I wasn't even sure what she was coming back to do or say, but the anger blazing in her eyes let me know that I had struck a nerve. She reached out and mushed me in the face hard as hell. "You only got a few more times to call me out my name before I do something to yo' ass that will have me smiling in my mugshot!"

I've never been hit by a woman in an argument, and my instincts kicked in at the wrong time. I was high, tipsy, angry, and my judgement was clouded. I moved so fast that I didn't even realize that my hand was around her neck until I was already squeezing. "Don't put your fuckin' hands on me. What the fuck is wrong with you?" I squeezed with all my might for about four seconds, and then I realized what in the hell I was doing.

I let Suzon go, and she began to cry as she walked away from me. I was still pissed, but I was out of pocket for that shit. I began to panic. I was pretty confident that me choking her wouldn't harm the babies in anyway, but I couldn't be too sure. Would she call the police? Would they arrest me for domestic violence? "Suzon." She kept walking.

I rushed after her and prevented her from opening the front door. I placed my body on hers as he we stood at the door. "I'm sorry. I'm sorry. I didn't mean to do that shit. I'm sorry."

"Please just let me go. Please." Her voice was hoarse, and I felt like shit.

"Suzon."

"Let me gooooooo," she couldn't even yell because her voice was scratchy and deep.

I did what she asked however and let her leave. Fuck!!

Suzon ♥

When I left Esai's house, in the Uber I texted Papi and told him that I was pregnant, and that we couldn't see each other anymore. I even sent him the money back. I was so angry that my hands were trembling. Of course, he had all kinds of questions, with the main one being who I was pregnant by. I simply blocked him because I was getting a headache, and I didn't have the energy for the shit I was going through. In my condo, I shed a few more tears, then I made myself woman up. I wasn't about to sit around and be sad over Esai's emotional bi-polar ass. Yes, I was wrong for dealing with Papi. But his triggered ass didn't give a damn about Big Draco. He had his panties in a bunch because his ex and his friend did him dirty, and that wasn't my problem. He wasn't about to emotionally abuse me any time that he got mad. Slut, hoe, bitch, those were all names my mother had called me in the past, and I wasn't letting anyone else do that shit. I was wrong for putting my hands on him. Domestic violence goes both ways, but I was dumb to think I could co-parent smoothly with someone that I didn't know. Our shit had become toxic fast as hell.

I was almost grateful for my blow up with Esai because it created a monster. For the next few days, no matter how bad I felt, I woke up and did my hair and make-up. It was just like playing dress up. I had to take advantage of being able to still fit my clothes and that was a stretch because my ass was getting so big, but I used it to my advantage. I was going to take mad pictures as Mona suggested so I could post them all throughout my pregnancy. I hadn't checked my PO box in a minute, and I had mad promo to do, so I stayed busy with that. One day I was doing a skin care routine video, and I had to stop to throw up. I brushed my teeth and got right back to work. I had gotten a little lazy, but I was back on it, and it paid off. I even got an offer to do a hosting in South Carolina, and they sent me half the money up front that same day. I didn't need Esai or Papi. I was going to boss up on my own and take care of my kids on my own.

I even paid for and enrolled in nail school. It would be another month before I started, but I was still excited. Every time I posted a picture, I had niggas in my DM's. Everything from rappers, athletes, actors, boxers, to regular niggas. I was flattered. That's what I had always wanted. To be able to catch the attention of rich ass niggas, but I couldn't even do anything with them. My ass was outta the game for at least seven months, and I guess I really didn't mind. I had my fun for a minute but when Esai got mad, the things he said to me made me realize how men really feel about me. I couldn't even be mad or blame them because they were going off what I gave them to work with. People like Mona don't care what people say about her as long as she's jet setting, getting her money, having good sex, and just living life. Me on the other hand, those things were nice, but I liked the romance side of it too. I wanted to fall in love and for a man to love me back. Most people aren't looking for love though. I lucked up with Big Draco, and that luck ran out fast.

One morning, I had just finished my photoshoot for the day when I saw an interesting story on the blogs.

There were rumors that Mona, Bakari, and Esai had a threesome in Dubai. My heart slammed into my chest as I read the article. Esai was one of my least favorite people in the world, but that shit still hurt. Mona. I guess I shouldn't even have been shocked because Mona is just a hoe that loves dick and money, and I had played myself thinking she was a friend and that she would be loyal to me. The game was cutthroat like that. Maybe Esai was trying to prove a point. Maybe he wanted me to see how it felt for a person you deal with to have sex with your best friend. Maybe I deserved it. I couldn't dwell on that shit. Baby daddy or not, Esai didn't owe me shit. It would have been nice for Mona to show some type of loyalty, but she didn't, so it was whatever.

Ironically, thirty minutes after I read the story on the blog, Esai texted me and asked how I was doing. It had been five days since our argument at his house, and he hadn't asked me how I was doing in the past five days, so why now? I simply ignored him. He wasn't getting any of my time or my energy. Esai could really kiss my ass.

♥♥

I was going to get my hair done a few days later, and guess who I saw leaving out of the salon as I was approaching? Yeap. Ms. Mona. I know that you can't believe everything you read on the blogs, but the guilty expression on her face told me all that I needed to know. That shit stung just a little bit. I can't even lie. I was going to keep walking as if I didn't know her, but she stopped me.

"You're not even going to speak to me, Suzon?"

I frowned up my face and looked at her like she had two heads. "Speak to you for what? We haven't spoken since I invited you to Esai's game with me. We're both adults with our own lives, so you don't have to call or text me every day. But it says a lot that you didn't even call after that story broke. If it wasn't true, we could have laughed about the shit. You're something else, but I knew that already."

Mona kissed her teeth. "I flew out to Dubai with Bakari on a whim. We ended up hanging out with Esai one night, and I got too heavy handed with the coke. Between all the coke and the liquor, I don't even remember all that happened, but something about a threesome was mentioned. Esai wasn't with it though." I saw just a hint of shame flicker in her eyes. "He wanted no parts of it. Had he wanted to do it, I'm sure I wouldn't have said no just because I was super fucked up. It's like I wasn't even in my own body. I would never do that shit sober, but he's not even your man. You barely know him. You just accidentally got pregnant by him."

Her trying to justify herself to me was funny as hell. It was crazy that Esai had more loyalty to me than she did. Or maybe it wasn't even about loyalty. Maybe he just didn't want to have sex with her. Either way it went, I was over the conversation, and I was over Mona. She didn't have to worry about me ever again. I walked away from her and entered the salon to get my hair done. My jeans were already getting hard to button, and I was running out of time to be able to post full body pictures without wearing something to hide my stomach. I was going on three months and starting to look slightly bloated. I figured in a good four weeks maybe, I'd be showing. By that time, I would be busy with nail school. I was throwing up a little less, but I still didn't have a lot of energy. I was doing what I had to do though. Every day I was doing something to make money and I knew once I started doing nails, shit would be lit.

I spent two hours in the salon, then I headed to the grocery store to get some food. As I approached my condo, I was surprised as hell to see Papi in the hallway waiting for me. "What are you doing here?" I asked with furrowed brows.

His eyes fell down to my belly. I guess he thought he'd be able to see that I was pregnant. "How you just gon' block me though? Why didn't you answer any of my questions?"

I rolled my eyes as I juggled my bags in my hand and tried to open the door, and his rude ass didn't even offer to help. "Because the questions you were asking weren't any of your business, Papi. You're not the father, and that's all you need to know."

He followed me inside. "Suzon, we been fucking around for how long? You just up and block me like that? You with this nigga? What does being pregnant have to do with me and you?"

I narrowed my eyes and studied him intensely to see if his eyes were red or if he appeared to be under the influence of some kind of drug. "Are you high? I'm pregnant with whole ass twins and even if it was only one baby, I don't want to be having sex with you while I have someone else's kid in me. I did it once, and I didn't like the way I felt afterwards."

"Who are you pregnant by?" he asked with a little more bass in my voice like he was supposed to intimidate me.

I didn't want it to get out, and I hoped Papi wouldn't run his mouth. The shit would be out sooner or later though. "Esai from the Hornets, and I better not hear this shit repeated, or I'm blowing you up, Papi. I swear on everything."

Papi chuckled. "You went and got a lame ass ball player." His eyes widened with recognition. "Ohhh that's why that nigga was in your section that night. Well, at least you didn't move on with a broke nigga, huh?" he smirked.

"I didn't move on with anyone because we're not together. Getting pregnant was an accident not that it's any of your business. No one knows but me, him, and Mona, and I want to keep it that way," I shot him a warning glare.

He held his hands up in surrender. "I don't run my mouth. That's bitch shit. I guess you can take my man's pictures of your page now, huh?"

Papi was really starting to piss me off with all of his little slick comments. Men as a whole were beginning to make my skin crawl. "Nigga, did I take them off after I fucked you? If I need to take mine off, you need to take yours off. 'Cus your fraud ass damn sure don't be repping Big Draco when you be begging to see me."

"Me and Big Draco shared hoes all the time. This shit wasn't no different. Only thing is, he isn't alive for us to trade stories," he looked me up and down.

I wasn't going to put my hands on him like I had done Esai. "Get the fuck out. I'm such a hoe, but your married ass is over here acting pressed. Kick rocks lame ass nigga," I hissed, and Papi walked towards the door. "Fuckin' trick!" I yelled out after the door closed behind him.

At that moment, Esai called my phone, and I picked it up and threw it across the room. I just wanted niggas to leave me alone!

ESAI 🏀

I had pissed Suzon off something terrible because it had been three weeks since our argument, and she wouldn't talk to me. I was trying to respect her privacy and not pop up at her condo, but it didn't look like that was going to get me anywhere. She'd been posting regularly on social media, and I felt like a stalker. She seemed to get prettier with each post, and I regretted some of the things that I said to her. Finding out she had sex with Big Draco's friend was a trigger for me, but I couldn't compare her to Afrika, simply because she wasn't Afrika. Even though it was still wrong, she was right about one thing. Big Draco was gone, and he wasn't coming back. I knew I had to have some kind of respect for Suzon when Mona tried to fuck me in Dubai, and I turned her down. I was drunk as hell and had smoked some bomb ass weed. Mona is sexy as fuck, and I've heard from a few different people that her pussy is off the chain. But I couldn't fuck her simply because she was Suzon's friend. I was pissed at Suzon at the time, and I still couldn't betray her like that. That's how I knew that Afrika never gave a fuck about me. Not for real.

    I needed someone to talk to, so I headed to my parents' house. Two days after my argument with Suzon, I went to Dubai for eight days, and it was a much needed trip. I spent a lot of it drunk off my ass and high, but it also gave me a lot of time to rest my body and my mind.

I processed what happened with Tyrese and Afrika, and I truly promised myself to move on from it the best I could.

"Me and Bakari are about to go upstairs and have some fun. You want to join us? I love being double stuffed," Mona giggled like the true freak that she is.

I drained the liquor from my glass as I thought about what she said. Her eyes were glassy as hell from all the coke she'd been sniffing. When I didn't answer, she attempted to entice me further. "I get off on sucking one guy off while another is hitting me from the back."

My first three nights in Dubai, I spent with three different women. It didn't matter where I was in the world, I could get pussy with no problem. I knew Mona kept her indiscretions on the low, so there was a chance that Suzon wouldn't find out. I still couldn't do it though. I was staring in Mona's face, but it was Suzon's face that was flashing in my mind. "You in or not?" Bakari stood up and eyed Mona with a lustful gleam in his eyes. He was ready to get the party started.

"Nah, I'm good. You two have fun."

Mona shrugged and walked off. Even I was shocked that I had turned her down, but I didn't have to be pressed about pussy. There were thousands of women that I could sleep with. I had a lot of years to deal with Suzon, and I didn't want to keep getting on her bad side.

That night in Dubai flashed through my memory every day. I don't know how that shit got out to the blogs. Unless maybe Mona mentioned being there to one of her groupie ass friends, and they leaked the shit. When I pulled up at the house, my dad was outside cooking on the grill.

"Hey son. You're just in time for some tender steaks, some succulent chicken, and the best almost burnt hotdogs you've ever seen," he chuckled.

"That's what's up, pops. I'm going to holla at mom, and I'll be right back out."

I found my mom where I knew she'd be. In the kitchen. "What's up, ma?"

"Hey baby. I'm glad you stopped by. Your sister and the kids will be here in a minute. How are you doing?" My mother was pulling a pan of baked macaroni and cheese out of the oven.

"I'm good. I have some news though." I hoped I wasn't jumping the gun. Suzon wouldn't answer for me, but I didn't think she got mad and aborted the babies. My mom looked at me curiously. "In about six months or a little less, I'm going to have twins."

The way my mom looked at me like I was speaking another language made me chuckle. "Esai, stop playing."

"I'm serious, ma. After me and Afrika broke up, I was doing my thing. One night, a condom broke, she threw the plan B pill up, and the rest is history."

My mom's eyes widened. "Esai! Well, I mean I'm glad to be having grandbabies I guess, but you know you can't be out there sleeping around. It's not safe."

"I know ma. I'm being careful. I can't take anymore accidents."

"Who is this woman?"

"Her name is Suzon. She used to date a rapper that got killed. She's a popular social media influencer, and she makes money that way."

"Humph."

I pulled out my phone and went to Suzon's IG page. I showed my mother one of her more tasteful pictures. "Ohhh, she's pretty, Esai."

"Yeah, she is. When we can get along, she's cool,

but we're not speaking at the moment. It's kind of hard trying to co-parent with someone that you hardly know. We're going to have to make it work though."

"Yes, you are, and I want to meet her. The two of you might not be together, but my grandkids will not be referred to as an accident. I want to get to know her. Whatever is going on, make it right."

I gave a head nod and talked to my mom a little while longer. I stayed at my parents' house for about four hours, then I decided to pop up at Suzon's condo. She could get mad, she could even refuse to open the door, but I had to try. I was actually nervous as I headed into her building. I decided to give her a heads up when I was on the elevator. I texted her that I was at her door. By the time I reached her door, she was opening it. She gave me a perplexed look, but she didn't say anything. I walked inside her condo and took her appearance in. She was dressed in a white oversized shirt, and a small belly bump was visible underneath the shirt. Just seeing her face had me at a loss for words. I knew the kind of life that she used to live. I know the circumstances that we met under and after what Afrika did to me, I should have been guarded as hell, but Suzon had done something to me. Vibing with her on her birthday was easy. Talking to her, joking with her, it was nice. It was peaceful, and I wanted to get to know her more. And not just because she was pregnant by me.

"You just gon' stand there?" She had an indifferent look on her face like she didn't give a damn about me one way or the other.

"I'm sorry for how I came at you. You having sex with Papi was none of my business. The things I said to you were wrong, and I should have never put my hands on you. I didn't sleep with Mona. She tried, but I turned her down. I put that on my kids."

"She told me." Suzon shifted her weight from one leg to the other and looked away from me.

I stepped into her personal space and turned her face towards me. "It's still very early. There's still a lot we don't know about each other, but I want to get to know you. And not just because of the babies. Your birthday was one of the best and most genuine times I've had in a minute. I want more times like those. I will never call you out of your name again, and I for sure will never put my hands on you again."

Suzon didn't respond, and we just glared at each other for a moment. I placed my lips on hers and snaked my tongue into her mouth. I reached underneath her shirt and touched her firm belly. "They still giving you hell?"

"Not as much as they were. I had an ultrasound today."

She stepped back and walked over to the coffee table. "You found out the sex?"

She nodded. "Damn. How did you know I didn't want to be there?"

"I didn't really care."

"That's fair, I guess." She handed me the ultrasound, and I looked down at it. I saw the words on the pictures. "Two boys?"

She nodded. "Yeap. I didn't get my one of each, but it's cool."

I stared at the picture as I envisioned having two sons to play basketball with. I felt like I wasn't ready for kids but now that I had been thrown into it, I was actually looking forward to it. "You been thinking about names?"

"I kind of like Esai Jr. and Enai."

I looked from the ultrasound to her face. She had been mad at me, and she was still going to name one of the babies after me? That meant a lot to me, and I kissed her again. That time, I kissed her with more passion, and we ended up in her bed. I placed kisses from her neck all the way down to her belly. I placed my face between her thighs and sucked her clit into my mouth as she moaned. Since me and Afrika broke up, I'd had my share of women. I had some good sex and some not so good sex. I had some short conversations, and none of them had left an impact on me the way that Suzon had. I licked and sucked her into an orgasm and after she came, we kissed hungrily as I stroked her walls. She was so wet that it was insane. Suzon hands down had the best pussy that I had ever had in my life.

"You feel so fucking good," I moaned.

"Esai," she whimpered my name as her pussy muscles contracted on my dick, and she came for the second time.

I came with a loud grunt right behind her. I kissed her chin, her lips, her nose, and her forehead making her giggle.

"Did somebody miss me?'

"I did. What you said was right. I can be an asshole. I'm working on that though. Okay?"

"You're not that bad. Only when you get mad, and I have to take some of the blame. I did meet you on some hoe shit."

"We were both being hoes. I can't judge you. That's the past. We're in a different place now. I want us to get along regardless of whatever. I want to give dating a try if you're with it. I don't want us to rush. If it doesn't work, we still agree to co-parent in a healthy way. Cool?"

"Cool."

"And no more hiding. If the blogs see us there will be stories. You ready for all that?"

"I'm good."

I kissed her on the lips again. It was time to see just what would become of me and Ms. Suzon.

Suzon ♥

Seven months later...

I peeked at Esai Jr. and Enai as they slept peacefully in their cribs. My babies were so freaking cute. They had been born three weeks early, but they weighed four pounds each, and they were healthy. Esai stepped up to the plate in a big way and not only did we start dating, but he began to really fall in love with being a father. By the time I was six months pregnant, he had an entire nursery at his house. He even painted the walls and had a jungle theme going on. The size of the nursery in their dads' house was larger than my bedroom in my condo. They also had a closet full of clothes at his house and everything from highchairs, car seats, strollers, and walkers. Esai and I went out shopping for the babies for the first time when I was five months pregnant, and the rumors started. We confirmed them when I was on live one day, and he walked by the camera. We weren't in a relationship, but we were dating and taking things slow. We hadn't argued since he came back around and though I didn't admit it to him, I had fallen in love with him. I didn't ask him a lot of questions and if he was messing with groupies, I had no clue. I kept waiting for the day that I would find something out on the internet and be embarrassed but so far, that day hadn't come.

Esai came in the room. "You look good as hell. Damn." He smacked me on the ass, and I smiled.

"I don't want to leave them." I had on a black

dress that was tight as fuck and had black sequins all over it. My kids were seven weeks old, and I had my first hosting since they had been born. My popularity grew even more after people assumed I was with Esai, and I was getting $4,500 for this hosting. I was still going to do hostings every now and then, but ya girl is a certified nail tech. I finished school, and I'm in the process of opening my shop. The grand opening is in two months.

Esai spent two nights a week at my condo, and I spent two nights a week with him. He was watching the boys while I went to my hosting.

"It's only for a few hours." He walked up behind me and wrapped his arms around me. He then placed a kiss on the nape of my neck. "Don't get nobody fucked up tonight."

"Boy, please. My breasts are full of milk, and I just started back having sex with you. I'm not interested in anyone."

"Well, they'd be dumb as hell not to be interested in you. If anyone asks you if you're single, I want you to be able to tell them no. We've been taking it slow for months, and I want to be with you."

That caught me off guard. Though we had been getting along, I knew how Esai felt about relationships since Afrika did what she did. A part of me also felt like even though he respected me as the mother of his kids, he would always look at me sideways because of how we met. I loved Esai, but I didn't feel like he loved me back. We just got along well and had amazing sex.

"You're ready to be in a relationship?"

"I am. That running around sleeping with different women gets old after a while. Maybe I'm an old soul, but I want what my parents have."

I smiled at him. "I would love to be your

girlfriend." We shared a kiss, then I had to head out so the driver could get me to the club.

 On the way there, I couldn't stop smiling. I no longer hung with the crowd that I used to, but Esai's sister and I had become pretty close. I also had a very good relationship with his mom. I hadn't spoken to my mother since I blocked her, but it was all good. Maybe one day we would get it together but until then, I was happily protecting my peace. After Big Draco died, it was all about securing a bag for me. Falling in love didn't seem feasible, but I had been proven wrong and if I had to choose between the money or love, I'd choose love any day. Esai and my boys gave me what I had been missing, and that was better than all the weed, liquor, partying, money, and social media fame in the world. Hoes can have happy endings too!

Note from the author....

If you purchased this book then you may know the reason that I wrote it. I was sitting on the cover, but I hadn't started writing it yet. Fed 12, 2021 two weeks after my grandmother died, my 26 year old cousin was found outside at his apartment complex. His name was Jordan, but his mother simply called him Joy. He was her only child, and still a month later, my heart still aches for her. She had to get a knock on the door from the police telling her that her child was dead. He didn't have insurance, and I wanted to do something for my aunt, so at the spur of the moment, I decided to offer this exclusive book that wouldn't be available on amazon. I didn't want to ask for something for nothing, so I began working on this book. Within two hours of announcing this, I was able to send my aunt $500. The way my readers showed up and showed out for me, I appreciate you so much. I am a person of my word, and I want these books mailed out on April 1, so on March 14 at 12:19 am I am finishing this baby up. I didn't want to do a novella, but it isn't super long because I was working on a schedule. I didn't rush, and I hope you enjoy the story, because this is different for me. It's not street and gritty with a bunch of plot twists. What I am working on next, is back to that hood ish! Thank you all so much for supporting. I appreciate you always!!

Made in the USA
Middletown, DE
28 July 2024